T0114851

BESET

A NOVELLA

EDWARD RANIOLA

authorHOUSE®

AuthorHouse™
1663 Liberty Drive
Bloomington, IN 47403
www.authorhouse.com
Phone: 833-262-8899

© 2020 Edward Raniola. All rights reserved.

No part of this book may be reproduced, stored in a retrieval system, or transmitted by any means without the written permission of the author.

Published by AuthorHouse   10/22/2020

ISBN: 978-1-6655-0575-8 (sc)
ISBN: 978-1-6655-0574-1 (e)

Library of Congress Control Number: 2020921030

Print information available on the last page.

Any people depicted in stock imagery provided by Getty Images are models, and such images are being used for illustrative purposes only. Certain stock imagery © Getty Images.

This book is printed on acid-free paper.

Because of the dynamic nature of the Internet, any web addresses or links contained in this book may have changed since publication and may no longer be valid. The views expressed in this work are solely those of the author and do not necessarily reflect the views of the publisher, and the publisher hereby disclaims any responsibility for them.

—1—

Dim lights illuminate a wooden floor aged by spilled beer and dancing feet. The crowd is noisy and in good spirits. This is a bar for rockers. No collared shirts or dress shoes are necessary here. People come as they are. The fast-paced guitar riff complements the stomping of the bass drum and pounding of the snares.

Chord loves this place. He loves its people and music.

Chord Samson—he always has thought it a ridiculous name. His parents were musicians—young musicians—and he was their mistake. But like most mistakes, he's here for a reason. What does that say for anything not mistaken?

Chord is tall and lean; his face is chiseled and dark. He has thick dark hair and dark eyes that rest deep in their sockets. He sits in a dark corner booth with his best friend, Manny. They have fresh beers in hand, and a few empty glasses they've pushed to the back of the table wait to be picked up to continue their life cycle. *We all end up empty*, Chord thought, *praying to be used again.*

He knows that if someone asked Manny to define unhappiness, he'd just point his index finger, thumb up, at his own head and say, "This guy." He's actually quite

1

uplifting to be around, but Manny, like most people, measures his happiness by what he doesn't have. Yeah, he's out of shape, but he's by no means fat. He's a talented guy—an artist and a musician. The minute he's good at something, he runs from it.

Manny pulls his beer glass from his mouth after taking an enormous gulp and asks, "So what happened with Sara, man?"

Chord looks down at his glass and thinks, *Sara was amazing. She was beautiful, smart, and humorous, and she loved the shit outta me. It was going well, but I just didn't feel it. I really can't explain it. It was good.* Aloud to Manny, he says only, "I just wasn't ready to settle down yet."

"That's your fucking problem, man. You waste all of your good fortune."

Chord cringes inside when Manny lectures him. *What does he know?* he thinks. *He needs help.*

Manny continues. "You say you want to get married and have a family and a dog. White picket fence and all that shit. Then you have a perfect chick who can eventually provide all that, and you run from it."

Chord wants another drink. "I have to piss." He gets up and works his way through the crowd toward the bathroom, pondering the conversation. *It makes me sad—Manny telling me about me. When the advice you have for someone else suits you, you start to resent yourself.*

The bathroom is filthy. All of the drunk alpha males have marked their territory around the foot of the urinal. Trying to keep the bottoms of your pants clean and aim can be challenging when buzzed. Marker hieroglyphics act as a distraction as well. In blue over the urinal, someone has scrawled, "I pissed here." Someone else has written a response in black ink: "Glad you were able to figure it out, asshole!" On the stall door is an illustration of an enormous penis spraying some substance. Written in a different color of ink is a caption that reads, "In your mom's face."

These freestyle graffiti battles always make me laugh. Chord zips up his fly and leans down over the sink to rinse his hands. *I hate that there are no mirrors in this bathroom.*

At the booth, Manny orders another round for Chord and himself. A woman approaches Manny and sits across from him.

Manny looks at her, and she begins. "Hi. I was just curious about your friend. When he comes back, tell him Crystal—that's me—is waiting to talk to him at the bar."

Manny just nods without saying a word, and Crystal smiles and walks back to the bar. About a minute later, Chord returns and sits at the table, smiling at the waiting beer.

"That chick with the black skirt is Crystal. She wants you to talk to her," Manny says.

Chord looks over at Crystal, and she raises her glass slightly to indicate interest. "She's cute." Chord smiles and guzzles his beer. "You wanna get outta this place?"

"You're not going to talk to her?"

Chord looks at Manny and back to Crystal, thinking, *I don't know what to say to that. Does that make me an asshole? I just don't feel like talking to a chick tonight. Playing make-believe. Trying to talk over the music and gather some sense of who she is. This is a bar. I don't want to start talking about myself. Selling myself. Overemphasize the few good qualities I have so I don't seem inadequate. When I meet someone new,*

I can't figure out if I'm trying to justify my worth to her or to myself.

Chord replies to Manny, "She isn't my type."

With the night almost gone, Chord and Manny leave the bar. Chord takes a deep breath of urban air and smiles with love for the city. He looks at the buildings of brick joined with gray cement sidewalks and more graffiti— words and pictures with meaning only to a select few. The homeless, basking in the scent of their own urine, find solace under their flattened cardboard boxes. Drunk men and women stagger and curse their way to the next bar. All types of people are caught up in the same battle, fighting it in their own way. The Mohawks, tattoos, lovers, piercings, colored hair and nails, outfits made of God knows what kind of materials—all are mixed, matched, and scattered about this urban Shangri-la, all in search. Maybe Chord's not such a mess here. Maybe he doesn't have to be confused or scared. Maybe not.

The next morning, Chord awakens in Manny's house. There's something soothing about a couch converted into a bed after a night of drinking. It's temporary.

His face is coated with oil, a gift from his Italian ancestors. His mouth is pasty, and his head is flirting with an ache. Chord folds the used sheets and positions the pillows back neatly on the couch. He leaves without waking Manny.

Chord sits in his car in front of Manny's house and remembers waking up at Manny's when they were kids. It was the same routine, minus the bar and insightful conversations about life. It's a bit sad when you wake up and, suddenly, you aren't a child anymore. The big concern isn't what game you're going to play or whose house you're going to play at. You've traded in your bicycle for a leased car. You have bills. You've traded fights with your mom about brushing your hair for insecurity and expensive gel. You've traded in dreams of the future and what you will become for resentment. Chord drives off.

Manny listens to Chord leave, and once Chord is gone, he rolls out of bed and heads to the bathroom. Manny looks at himself in the mirror. He's wearing only boxer shorts, and he glares at his stomach, which flops over the front of the elastic waistband. He grabs hold of his stomach with both hands and jiggles it with a look of disgust in his eyes. He examines other parts of his body and face, which equally disturb him. Manny starts the shower.

After his shower, as Manny finishes buttoning his jeans, he looks at the mirror on his desk. Stuck in the bottom corner is a picture of himself with several other people in a clothing store. They are all wearing name tags. They are Manny's coworkers. He gently swipes his index finger over the female coworker standing next to him in the picture. His eyes gaze adoringly as he says, "Today's the day."

Manny walks briskly into the clothing store, greeted by Doug, who's working the register. Manny waves and walks into the back room for employees only. Steph and James are digging through boxes of new merchandise. Manny loves Tuesdays. Tuesday is the night when most of the employees work to restock all the new merchandise without distraction from the consumers. It's the time when he gets to spend the most time with Eloise.

"Hey, Manny, we have a load of new merchandise!" Steph exclaims with enthusiasm. "It's going to be a long night. Why don't you start opening the boxes of shoes?"

"Okay. Who else is working tonight?" Manny asks.

"It's just going to be us. Doug is going to do a double to cover.

Manny's heart drops, but he tries to keep a smile on his face. "Oh damn, that sucks for him. What happened to El?"

"Some surprise night her fiancé planned for her. She called me yesterday."

"Oh, cool." Manny walks to the back corner, where the boxes of shoes are. He feels a burning anger within.

"That guy has got it bad. It's kinda sad," James whispers to Steph.

"I know, right? I mean, the girl is engaged, for goodness sake."

Employment—the majority's source of unhappiness, the evil errand needed to sustain social acceptance. Chord hates his job. Or maybe he thinks too much in comparisons. Or it's the uniform. The fake smiles. The forced belief that they are heroes and are important, not harassing the public but doing their duty. It's all bullshit. But that must be how everyone feels about his or her job.

Chord isn't disliked within the precinct, but he's not really liked either. He is quiet and does what he has to do. The cop relationships displayed in the movies don't apply to Chord. He prefers it that way—not that he believes he's better than any other officer; he just doesn't want to find common ground.

Chord sits in the passenger seat of a police car. He's

distant and dreaming. His partner's last name is Stolsky. He drives aimlessly. Chord has recently started working patrol, which is to say he's one step above rookie status. Stolsky's regular partner was switched to a different tour, or shift, and Chord hasn't completely figured him out yet. They listen to the radio—central—waiting for a chance to use their power. Or maybe to help someone in need. One never quite knows.

The radio blares a call sign, or sector—a portion of a police precinct that a patrol car patrols for the day. More invisible boundaries. More freedom taken. Weak with power. There are multiple sectors assigned daily to cover a precinct. The one central now calls is Chord's.

"Sector John, EMS is requesting a patrol car for a DOA."

John is the sector. Each sector consists of smaller portions labeled by letters of the alphabet. Phonetically speaking, portion J, or sector J, is John. Everyone knows what DOA is an acronym for.

Chord and Stolsky pull up at the scene. There is an ambulance parked in front of a small house. The house was left to die years ago. Weeds are overgrown and invading all the walkways. The roof is sunken in, ready to collapse. The windows are broken and covered in plastic. Inside, a smell lingers. It is stale. Roaches have free roam and don't scurry when Chord enters. This is their house.

The EMS crew are in the back room and call for Chord and Stolsky. Lying in a bed faceup is an old woman. Her chin is sunken into her face like the roof of the house. Her eyes have dried with a plastic glaze like the windows. All the blood has pooled up inside her, settling in the backs of her legs and her back.

Chord stops and looks at the dead person. Maybe she's

someone's grandma. Someone's mother. Someone's sister. Now she's alone and dead. All he can think of is the amount of paperwork he's going to have to do. He'll have to find some way to contact the family. He feels not an ounce of caring for the lost soul. He's cold.

The mailman called the police because he noticed the mail hadn't been picked up for a week, and he knew that an elderly woman resided there. *Our hero.*

Apparently, the dead woman was a collector. The home contains all sorts of trinkets. They are all polished and standing erect in their display cases. Her costume jewelry glimmers in its little box as roaches crawl around it. She has dozens of boxes filled with pictures of another life—one in which she had children she loved and a husband. Smiling pictures. Party pictures. Pictures of vacations. Pictures of weddings. Pictures of all the people who let her die alone in a roach-infested, broken-down, stinky old house. The life has been sucked out of her wrinkled body, and her priceless treasures—trinkets of hope, of existence—couldn't buy her family's attention. Chord wonders if that's how he'll die. He feels the suffocating sense that time is running out for everyone.

Stolsky is getting anxious. "Let's get the fuck outta here. Old bag has no family. Let's wait in the car for the medical examiner." Stolsky is all heart.

Chord and Stolsky thank the EMS crew and go out to the patrol car to wait for the medical examiner.

Stolsky snores loudly. It reminds Chord of his father. Stolsky's mouth is wide open as his head slumps into the car seat headrest. He's not even thirty-five, and he's overweight, with a heart ready to explode. *First impressions*, Chord thinks.

Chord looks away and peers through the passenger window, thinking about his father. His musician dad was a successful failure. But he was an exceptional dad. His mom told him that after his father's music career failed to spread from their one-bedroom apartment, he lost hope and took a civil servant job. Then they had Chord and agreed on his name.

Chord can't fathom the idea that raising a child after failing to succeed in your dream makes you responsible. He doesn't want to have kids. Chord's father always pushed him to become a police officer or postal worker—any civil servant job. Chord battled but eventually succumbed to the life his father wished for him. It was as though Chord wasn't good enough for anything else. He had no higher hopes.

The medical examiner's truck pulls up, and Chord leaves Stolsky sleeping to deal with the ME.

Finally, it's Chord's favorite part of the day: leaving work. Chord drives a newer-model sedan. It takes him about forty minutes to get home. Without traffic, it would take twenty minutes. His eyes are tired and distant. He thinks out loud, saying, "Sometimes if you focus on the sound of the traffic hard enough, you hear the ocean."

He lives with his parents in a nice house with two floors. Pictures of anything music-related litter the walls—masochistic reminders of failure. Lately, every time Chord looks at the photos, he feels pity for his parents.

Chord's parents are waiting in the kitchen. His father is reading the newspaper, coffee is brewing, and his mother stands at the stove. They both smile when Chord enters. Chord's father is a clean-cut older man with gray hair. His mother is slender and tall, with long dark hair that almost reaches her waist. She asks Chord what he wants for breakfast. Chord sits and places his order.

"Did your father show you what he made?" Chord's mother, in between frying eggs, reaches for what appears to be a wooden frame. "He made it yesterday."

It's a picture frame made from wood in the shape of a music note. It holds a picture of Chord's dad in uniform when he was a young policeman, alongside a picture of Chord in uniform—past combined with the present. It's everything the old man could've hoped for. Their mirrored failures are sealed in a musical note. *Harmony.*

"What can I say?" Chord exclaims with a big smile. "How awesome! Wow, we look identical. And the note. How did you carve the note so well?" He places the frame on the counter to overlook their breakfast.

His dad relishes in his achievement. It makes him sad. Chord loves his parents.

Chord's father looks at Chord and then back to his music-note picture frame. His smile slightly buckles, and his eyes seem to be capturing another image.

Chord's dad thinks back to his old apartment. He's in his midtwenties. He sits at a desk, writing music. A guitar leans against the table. His head bobs up and down with the inaudible music he's imagining. The youth in his face emits happiness. With the flush of a toilet, Chord's young mom steps out of the bathroom and stands over Chord's father.

Her face is grave and pale with fear. She whispers, "I'm pregnant."

Chord's father's face wilts. He looks down at the notepad he is writing in and at his guitar. His body is frozen. He knows he needs to respond, but he can't control any part of himself.

"Say something," she says.

He looks up, desperate, "Isn't there a way to stop it?" He instantly regrets the response. "I mean, in the future, yes, I want to have children. I want it to be with you! But this is no good. My music is getting better and better. I'm meeting with the record guy. This is a big chance for our future!"

"You, you, you!" Chord's young mother points at her midsection, at the future Chord. "This is our future!"

Back in the present, Chord's father looks back at Chord eating his eggs, and his smile returns.

Stolsky pulls into his driveway. He quietly exits his vehicle and enters the front door of his house. It's a small house with three bedrooms. The lawn is green and trimmed. There is a swing hanging from a tree. Stolsky places his bags down on the dining room table. He moves into the kitchen and reaches into the refrigerator. He pulls out the milk and eggs. He grabs a mixing bowl and some pancake mix. While he's cracking eggs, his youngest daughter sneaks up behind him and hugs his leg.

"Hey there, sweetie! Did you have a good night sleep?"

The little girl nods. She's about four years old, with curly brown hair.

"Are your sisters awake?"

She smiles and shakes her head.

"Are you sure?"

Just then, his two other daughters charge into the kitchen, screaming and laughing. Stolsky screams out in make-believe fear and grabs them all in his arms. He kisses them all repeatedly all over their little faces.

Stolsky's daughters sit at the kitchen table, watching their father finish cooking breakfast. As he begins to serve the pancakes, his wife enters the kitchen in her flannel pajamas. "Something smells good." She smiles at Stolsky.

Their daughters, in unison, exclaim, "Daddy's making pancakes!"

"Oh, I see that! Yummy!" Stolsky's wife leans over and kisses his face. She grabs a plate of pancakes and places it on the table.

Stolsky is a different man when he is around his family. He is alive, as if the energy of his children and their love fuels him. He sits at the table, and the family eat their breakfast.

Afterward, Stolsky's wife finishes cleaning the dishes from breakfast with the help of her daughters as Stolsky steps out of the shower. He dries himself off and wraps his lower body in a towel. He looks at himself in the mirror, at his stomach. He sucks it in and lets it out. He knows he's overweight. Sometimes life gets too busy to focus on yourself.

From the other room, Stolsky's wife calls out to him. "The girls and I are leaving! We're going to be late for school!"

Stolsky runs down the stairs in his towel, grabs his girls, and hugs them, wishing each of them a good day at school. He kisses his wife and watches them load into the minivan.

When she backs out of the driveway, Stolsky goes back up to his bedroom, puts on underwear, and climbs into bed.

Manny is just arriving home from work. He has a defeated look on his face. He looks down at his wrist and grabs it with the other hand, squeezing his nails into his skin. He grunts and releases his grip. His wrist has indentation marks from his nails. It looks as though some wild animal bit him without breaking the skin. He takes a few breaths and exits his car.

Manny enters his house, and his mother is at the table, eating breakfast. "Where were you?"

Manny looks at her as though she is vile. "At work. What do you think?"

"Well, do you want breakfast?"

"No." Manny walks by her and heads up the stairs to his room. He slams the door to his room and punches at the air inside. "Fat, ugly loser!" He pulls at his shirt, trying to tear it from his body. The threads snap and pop, but he doesn't have the strength to tear the shirt completely. He exhausts himself and is left with only a drooping shirt and sadness.

His phone vibrates. It's Eloise. Manny sits on his bed with a feeling of exhausted joy and surprise. The text message reads, "Hope you guys weren't too busy last night! I probably would have had more fun at work! Hehe!"

Manny responds instantly, "You didn't miss much, but we missed you!"

Another night of aimless driving commences. They're trapped within their assigned borders, with Stolsky behind the wheel and Chord waiting for a job from central.

Two hours pass. Stolsky's and Chord's eyes grow heavier. "This is bullshit! I'm parking!" exclaims Stolsky. The soft nature he exhibits with his family has turned coarse and abrasive. The car pulls into a parking lot. It circles once and parks deep in the back corner of the lot.

Just as Stolsky's mouth falls open, central blares over the radio: "Shots fired. Two, three, and fourth. That's two, three, and fourth. Shots fired."

Stolsky pops up, complaining, "Just closed my fucking eyes! Probably a bullshit call!"

Over the radio, the sergeant asks central how many 911 calls were put in for the shots fired, and central responds that there were multiple calls. Stolsky screeches out of the parking lot. Chord turns on the lights and siren, and they speed down the empty midnight street.

They soon arrive on the scene. Chord and Stolsky come out of the car with their firearms drawn. A fifteen-year-old boy is sitting up against the front of a bodega, holding his face. Blood streams through his fingers from a large open wound. About ten feet away from him, lying facedown on the sidewalk, is a lifeless body of another boy about the same age. As Chord approaches, he notices a deep hole in the back of the boy's head and multiple wounds in the boy's back. *Shots fired.*

Stolsky screams at the onlookers to try to figure out who shot the boys and which way the perpetrators went. Finally, one of the dead boy's friends says they were walking on the sidewalk, when two more guys ran up on them and shot their friend. The witnesses are screaming in anger and sadness. One punches the walls, while others just stand in shock.

Other cops arrive, and the scene is blocked off. The boy must've been known in the neighborhood, because the mother of the victim already has been notified of her son's death, and she comes charging down the street, screaming. Chord stands frozen except for his pounding heart. Everything seems muffled and slowed down. Then it all swooshes back to regular speed, and he almost covers his ears.

That morning, before Chord leaves the precinct, he stops by the detective's office, or, as they call it, the squad. He knocks gently on the door, and a voice from inside calls out for him to enter. The office is a large room with desks lined against the walls, large filing cabinets, and a printer.

Detective Bradley sits at his desk, typing on his keyboard. "What's up, kid?"

"I was just curious if there was any further info about the shooting." Chord is hesitant.

Detective Bradley speaks while he types. "Yeah, it was gang shit. Poor bastard wasn't even the right kid. Sometimes you just don't get dealt a good hand."

"Jesus. Both of the kids were good kids?"

The detective stops typing and looks up at Chord. "I wouldn't say they were *good* kids. They didn't deserve what they got, though. I mean, the kid was shot four times. One bullet hit him in the leg, and then three more shots hit him: two in the back and one in the head. Fucking animals. Then they sliced that other kid. I mean, fifteen and sixteen. At that age, I was masturbating into a sock that my mom washed when she did the laundry. Times are changing."

Chord soaks in the information for a moment. "Any leads?"

"No, kid. No leads. No cameras in the area, no witnesses—no nothing. No one would tell us even if they knew something. Bullshit street nonsense. Everyone wants to complain about brutality, but no one wants to help. I have a lot to do. Why don't you apply for the squad if you're so interested?"

"Of course. Thanks for the info. Sorry to bother you."

Chord's face is blank. Numb, he drives like a robot with a destination programmed in his brain: home. Thoughts flood his mind. *I just don't understand this world we're living in. So full of hate. Just kids. Hating each other over nothing. Hate the president. Hate war. Hate peace preachers. Hate the opposite sex. Hate a different race. Hate a different religion. "I hate" is just another way to say, "Look at me; I need attention."* Then Chord speaks aloud to himself: "I hate my job. Hypocrite. I hate myself."

Chord arrives home from work at the usual time, welcomed by the usual routine. Breakfast is cooked. Chord and his parents sit together to eat, when his mother asks if something is wrong.

Something wrong? Chord thinks. *She hasn't a clue. I'd like to wipe the phony smile off my face and tell my parents that my life isn't a peachy wonderland of smiles and rainbows. Tell them I'm tired of playing make believe. I'm tired of being cordial with my coworkers. I'm tired of breathing and waking up in the morning. But what good would that do for me?*

Chord smiles an empty smile and says, "I'm just tired. I had a long night."

Chord finishes his coffee, cleans off his plate, and excuses himself. The shower runs hot, steamy water. The ceiling above is weathered and peeling. Chord undresses and steps into the porcelain cloud of steam, his sanctuary, a steamy secret world away from reality—alone. Chord slowly enters the stream of water. At first, the heat is slightly unbearable, but it soon becomes a liquid massage. Chord rests both hands on the shower wall and then his forehead. The water runs down the center of his back. His hands begin to shake, and then he begins to sob. He tries to control his emotions and not make too much noise.

Chord's mind races. *I am my own worst enemy. This is my sorry routine. I cry for all the people I miss. I cry for the kids shot to death for no reason. I cry for all the chances I didn't take. I cry because I have no idea who I am. I cry because I blame my parents. I cry because I'm a phony. I need to do something. I'm tired of having nothing to believe in. Nothing to look forward to. Why should I eat healthy or work out? Why should I save for my dad's future? What future? The human race is a matador, and Earth is the bull, slowly being bled out until the final nuclear thrust.*

An enormous pine tree stands staring at Chord, taunting him, challenging him. It's a tree any kid would attempt to climb. Its limbs are close together, forming a natural ladder. Chord stands at the base and stares up at it. His neck tilts back. He begins to climb.

He climbs with an unusual intensity, as if to prove to the tree he is unafraid and will not be bullied. After minutes of rapid climbing, Chord stops and looks up only to find there is no sign of the top. Disheartened, he takes a second to consider whether it's worth climbing more.

Chord hears music in the distance. It's the sound of an acoustic guitar, along with a woman laughing. The sound eerily grows more acute. Chord looks through the pine needles at a hole in the tree. He sees his father as a young man sitting in a metal folding chair with a guitar on his lap. His father strums a beautiful melody while the young version of his mother watches. Chord is in disbelief. They are beautiful together. His father can't be any older than Chord is now as he serenades Chord's mom, with both of them miniaturized in the tree. Chord's father finishes playing and tells his future wife, "I'm gonna make it, babe. I can make it." Chord is seeing his father for the first time as a man full of hope, not broken by life.

Chord hears a noise below and looks down past his feet. The branches have all become brittle or broken, making it impossible to climb back down. He looks back into the hole and finds it empty.

He looks up. "I can make it," he says aloud to himself. He starts climbing again while repeating to himself, "I can make it. I can make it." With his left hand, he feels a wet, mushy substance on the branch. Smeared on the palm of his hand is a wet chunk of clotted blood. The branch itself is coated with clotted blood.

Chord climbs past the blood only to find the young gunshot victim staring down at him. The victim's pale dead eyes follow Chord's movement. Chord's heart fires blood through his body so fast he almost passes out. *I will not be deterred*, he thinks. *I can make it.* He gathers himself and starts to climb slowly past the living corpse.

Just as Chord reaches the same level as the dead boy, the boy screeches, "I can make it!" Chord loses grip and falls.

Chord feels as though he is falling in slow motion. He hears the melody of his father's guitar. At the base of the tree, he sees all the cops from his precinct laughing and holding their arms up to catch him.

Chord's eyes open. *Dreams. Nightmares.* It's only twelve in the afternoon. *I need to sleep.* Chord's room is bright from daylight blaring through the blinds covering his windows. *Useless fucking blinds.*

The TV in the other room regurgitates news of war and the horrible decisions of the president. It spews rumors of the upcoming presidential candidates, children abducted, elderly people beaten, car accidents, drunk drivers, global warming, death and destruction, harsh weather, lies, winning lottery numbers, and celebrity couples parting. Chord covers his face and ears with his pillow, clenching down like a vise grip around his head. *If there is a God, he must be hard of hearing.*

It's no use. Chord can't sleep. Every sound is another reason to wake up. For more than twenty years, he has been conditioned to sleep when the sun sets. *This is crazy. What kind of job has you working through the night?* Chord rolls around his bed, gradually coiling the sheets around his torso, until his movement is restricted. Frustrated and helpless, he kicks wildly to free himself. *I can't take this shit much longer! Sometimes it feels like we wrap ourselves in the sheet of life, and then it suffocates us. Every decision is just another toss and turn.*

Chord quietly, with great frustration, says out loud, "God, just let me fall asleep and never wake up." He desperately flails his arm, smashing his elbow through the wall.

From the other room, Chord's mother yells, "What the hell was that?"

Chord doesn't answer. He pulls his arm from the gaping hole and examines his bloody elbow.

"Chord! What are you doing in there? Are you punching things again?"

Chord answers that he is fine and just banged his arm in his sleep. He gets out of bed and dresses himself. Then he leaves the house.

"Fuck! Fuck! Shit! God dammit!" Chord speeds down the expressway in his sedan. His eyes are wild with an array of emotions. "I can't take this shit anymore. I just wanna go to sleep. Everything's in chaos." He almost sideswipes the guard rail as he fishes his cell phone from his pocket. "I'm taking off tonight. I can't do this. Fuck! This job is making me crazy. No money! Debt! Small paychecks. Living at home. American dream my ass!"

During his wild, speeding rant, Chord can't help but think of Heather.

The first time he saw her was in a club. Chord didn't want to be there, but he was. Manny and a few other guys had dragged him along. Anyway, he was there. They were all drinking and having a good time. The club was so crowded one could barely take a step in any direction. Chord was mingling with Manny, when he first made contact with Heather, out of all the people crammed into the small club; all the similar faces, shirts, and pants; and all the long-haired women with cocktails. She entered.

It was as if he could no longer control his eye movement. His eyes stayed fixed on her. She floated through the crowd, untouched, unique. She placed her jacket on the couch, along with many others.

Chord turned to Manny and told him, "That is the girl I'm going to marry."

She was beautiful. Her hair was pin straight and glimmered with health. Her skin was smooth, and her lips were succulent. She was encapsulated by a globe protecting her from the uniform look of everyone else. God, how he wanted to meet her. Instantaneously, he was addicted. He felt that one glance from her could cure the unhappiness of the world.

Chord started to doubt himself. He thought he'd have no chance with a woman of that magnitude, but then they met. Chord summoned the courage and sat next to her and began a conversation. He never had dreamed he had it in him, but at the end of the night, they kissed and exchanged numbers.

Chord speeds down the road. "She was the one all right. The one to destroy the last ounce of hope I had for any meaning of the word *love*. In four simple words, she collapsed any sense of adequacy or self-worth I thought I had: 'Love is not enough.'" That was her answer to Chord's proposal and the last time he saw her.

Chord punches the steering wheel, causing the horn to wail. His sedan races down the expressway, crying out for unwanted attention. Chord tears the top of the steering wheel off, and the horn goes silent. The car continues on, speeding away from the hole in the wall. Away from the hole in his heart. Away from the twenty-year retirement sentence. Away from the projected failures he sees in his father. Away from all the wasted childhood dreams and phony movie romances. Away.

Chord's eyes begin to feel the lack of sleep as he passes the Welcome to New Jersey sign on the interstate. *Half the time, we don't even know what we're running from. We just run.*

A couple hundred feet ahead, Chord notices a few tractor trailers parked in the shoulder along an exit ramp. He pulls his car to the side of the road and tucks it safely behind one of the trailers. The fuel gauge displays a red needle pointing at a letter *E*. *We all eventually end up running on empty.* That little *E* was just another boundary. Another reason to quit. Another reason to go back to his sector job and sector home, the precinct of life. Chord reclines, and his eyes close with ease.

Chord wakes up in his room to the sound of an engine running outside. The idle engine must be parked in the driveway, because Chord can feel its vibration. He looks out his window and sees a tractor trailer parked across his front lawn.

He gets out of bed and exits his room. He fumbles through the darkness of his house toward the front door. He exits into the muggy night. His eyes struggle to adjust to the lights of the truck. The air reeks with a stale odor. Chord walks over to the truck. "What are you doing on my front lawn?"

An eerie female voice answers, "I think I hit something."

Chord notices a lump of something lying in front of the truck. It's a lump of clothes. As Chord approaches the lump, he realizes it's a human body.

"Ma'am I think you hit someone!" Chord turns and looks through the windshield. Behind the steering wheel, illuminated by the dashboard lights, is the DOA woman. Her eyes have a plastic glaze, and her mouth is open; she begins to cackle.

Then a voice from behind Chord exclaims, "I'm fine, mister!"

Chord jumps around, and the lump in the street is the gunshot victim. The boy's dead eyes stare at Chord while he speaks. Brain matter and blood fall from the gaping hole in his head.

Chord screams and runs toward his house, which he sees is the old woman's broken-down, roach-infested house. Over the loud cackling, the dead boy moans, "I had dreams too!"

Chord cries out as he falls to his knees, holding his ears. A loud knocking in his head seems inescapable.

Knock! Knock! Knock!

Chord sits up and hits his head on his rearview mirror. A highway patrol cop stands at the side of his car. "You can't stay parked here." The tractor trailer is just pulling off from the shoulder.

"I'm sorry." Chord gathers his senses. "I'm leaving. Sorry."

The highway cop walks back to his vehicle as Chord starts his engine. Chord rubs his eyes, which are still moist from tears. "What an ass." He looks at his watch. It's nine o'clock at night. "I can still make it to work."

Butterflies begin their lives ugly. No one ever shares in the beauty of a caterpillar inching by. Caterpillars become beautiful. Children are different. Children begin their lives beautiful.

Unique. Full of hope. Over time, children are cocooned by social ideals. They become ugly. They become scarred adults with no room for inspiration.

Chord, after making it on time to work, stares at a caterpillar inching along the windshield wiper of the patrol car. His eyes are heavy from lack of sleep. Stolsky is sleeping wide-mouthed next to him. The radio is silent. Silence has a way of opening parts of the subconscious that will drive you crazy.

Chord's eyes focus past the caterpillar and out into the street at the drunk couples stumbling from place to place. "I'm so tired." Chord sees the gunshot boy peek his bloody head out from the edge of a building, causing him to flinch.

Stolsky wakes up. "What's up? We got a job?"

"No. Go back to sleep."

He doesn't need to tell Stolsky twice.

Chord rubs his eyes and continues to peer out into the night. He's tired of dreaming of some better life he will never have, tired of living with all of his successful failures. *People are happy*, he thinks. *Maybe we want to believe people are happy because we want to be happy. I fear I will never allow myself to feel that way. I mean, we're all brought up to want more. Want, want, want. I want to meet the satisfied people. I want to know their secrets. I want to steal their happiness for myself.*

Chord and Stolsky enter the locker room. Stolsky has a wide smile on his face as he exclaims, "What a relaxing night! What did we answer—one job?" Stolsky chuckles.

All Chord can think of is how he wants to smack Stolsky's pathetic smile from his face. He thinks to himself,

Maybe if he had been up all night listening to the radio, he wouldn't be so damn cheery. Chord doesn't answer; he just makes a left down the row of lockers.

His eyes are deep and dark. His skin has a yellow glow. When he arrives at his locker, the combination of anger, fear, and lack of sleep overwhelms him. He opens his locker, carefully listening to make sure no one sees him in this personal moment. He pulls his gun from his holster and presses it against his temple. "I am the caterpillar."

He looks into the mirror hanging on his locker door— such a pathetic sight. Chord puts the gun down in his locker and takes a deep breath. He finishes getting dressed and begins to leave the locker room. The other officers are dressing themselves in front of their lockers. Chord looks at them with disdain. Fat, balding, wasted souls. He doesn't want to end up like this. Divorced. Cursed. Out-of-shape minds. Chord fears he's losing himself before he has even had a chance to find himself.

Chord sits in his room in front of his television. It's nine in the morning. Alongside his chair stand two empty beer bottles. He sits and stares at his reflection in the floor-to-ceiling mirrored closet door while drinking from a third half-empty bottle of beer. *It's not until your life is completely transformed from what you imagined it would be that you realize you have no place in it.*

Chord is breaking down and falling apart, destroying the simplicity he has created in order to re-create himself. *Doctors of the mind would prescribe medicine at this point*, he thinks. Chord can't help but feel an intense emptiness—a black hole in his chest that sucks every breath he takes from his lungs. His anger builds as his veins protrude.

"Suicide is such bullshit."

Chord swallows the rest of his beer. In his mirror, he sees himself when he was eight. He blinks and rubs his eyes, but still, there is his eight-year-old self peering back in the mirror. The happiness he sees in himself is unbearable. *What happens from eight to twenty-eight? Is it knowledge that turns us into caterpillars? That forbidden fruit that first allowed evil into our world?*

Chord's chest feels heavy with secret emotions the world can't handle or understand. He pops another beer open, turns his television on, and starts drinking. The floor above him creaks, and then he hears the sound of footsteps. His parents have awoken.

Chord's mother works at the stove, cooking breakfast. "I'm worried about Chord. He seems so unhappy."

"He's fine. He's just growing up."

"There are seven beers missing from the refrigerator. He's becoming an alcoholic. And he is punching things again. I found another hole in his wall."

Chord's father doesn't want to hear it. "He'll be fine. You worry too much." Chord's father sits back in his chair. A familiar feeling creeps into his heart. His fingers tingle as the melody of his guitar disturbs his thoughts. He excuses himself to go to the bathroom.

Chord's father enters his bedroom, and instead of going to the bathroom, he enters his closet. After carefully assembling a makeshift ladder, he pulls an old acoustic guitar down from the attic hatch in his closet. He holds it in his arms as one would hold a lost child found. He sits and gently strums a soft melody. He grabs a small pad and pencil and jots down the notes of the melody. He wonders if Chord feels the same sadness he did at Chord's age.

Chord's mother stands over the oven, motionless, as if she's recharging some internal battery. She could've been a businesswoman with a college education. The day she found out she was pregnant was the last day of the life she'd dreamed of, the death of her eight-year-old self. *Do we all have a hidden passion? A dream we fear to imagine as real? Are all of us struggling with an emptiness we dare not attempt to fill?*

Chord is alone with his beer. His dad is alone with his melody. His mother is alone with her aspirations. All are together in the same lonely house with the same lonely condition.

Chord wakes to the sound of his mother knocking on his bedroom door. "Chord, don't you have work?"

A sharp pain reverberates throughout his head as he moans an almost incomprehensible "No." He glances over at his chair, which is surrounded by empty beer bottles. His television is on mute. He realizes he does have work tonight, but he doesn't care.

He thinks to himself, I'm not a cop. *I'm not sure what I am. How do we know who we can be if we don't ever take the risks we are raised to fear? I am not going to be just another product of my upbringing, the proud clone of my failed parents. In the end, I will take the path that most frightens me. That is the only way I can save them from a life of failed aspirations. That is the only way I can save myself.*

Marriage, security, children—these are the hopes his parents have for him, their idea of his "normal" life. *Add a white picket fence, and you have an American fantasy.* It's just as unrealistic as his father's desire to become a famous guitarist and his mother's aspiration to become a wealthy businesswoman.

The human condition has destroyed this country. In fact, the human condition is destroying this world. Why am I expected to keep up with the status quo? The world our parents knew is dead. My hope is dying. Chord pulls the electrical cord of his alarm clock until it detaches from its source of power and flails loosely in his grasp. He drops it and rolls onto his other side, falling back to sleep.

Chord wakes to his cell phone vibrating. *Work. AWOL. Suspension.* Chord answers the phone.

On the other end of the line, his sergeant begins his smart-ass-rhetorical-question routine. "Well, well, Samson, how nice to hear from you. Were you planning on coming in to work tonight? Did you over sleep? Drink too much?"

Chord hates sarcasm. "Sir, I overslept. Would it be all right for me to take the night off?"

After a long groan, the sergeant grants Chord the night off.

Chord gets out of his bed, still dressed from the previous night and day, and leaves his house.

It's midnight. His car basically drives itself to the bar. Alcohol is refuge for self-destruction. The bar is wild. The music is electric. Chord finds an empty chair at the far end of the bar. No matter how many lonely people there are in this city, it always seems easy to find a chair separate and alone in the corner of a bar. Chord settles in and attempts to allow the music to ignite is mood.

After an hour at the bar and a few beers, Chord realizes the music isn't going to give him the boost he hoped for. Once you've predetermined how you want to feel, it's hard to allow for a mood alteration. Chord orders a shot of vodka with his next beer and then goes to the bathroom. The same graffiti battle resides on the stall door. The graffiti instructions above the urinal are still present. There are a few new additions. Chord pulls a pen from his pocket and decides to add his own contribution.

Scrawling on the bathroom door for all to see as they exit, Chord writes, "Happiness is camouflage for despair."

As Chord walks back to his chair, he notices a beautiful woman with vibrant blue eyes sitting in it. She's holding a glass of white wine and displaying a warm smile. As Chord walks toward her, she glances upward and locks in on him. She giggles as Chord approaches.

"This must be your seat?" There is friendliness and warmth in her every action.

"Yeah, that was my seat."

She smiles. "So you're saying it's not anymore?"

"I'm saying that if I were to attempt to move you and sit there again, the chair itself would smack me."

She laughs.

Chord starts to think that maybe taking off work was a good idea. "So are you here alone?"

"Actually, I am, but I'm waiting for—and there he is." She gestures toward the door at a tall man in a black suit.

"Oh, I'm sorry."

She giggles. "Why are you sorry? I stole your seat. And I thank you for letting me use it while I waited."

"Well, I thank you for keeping it warm." Chord smiles as she gets up and, with her wine, leaves to greet her friend.

Chord sits down, and his smile melts into a bitter look of resentment. He watches as the woman opens her arms wide and embraces the lucky suit. Chord concludes that the man in the suit probably makes a load of money—probably works as an investment banker or trader or in some other lucrative profession—and she would just perceive Chord as a waste of time. *Love is not enough.*

Chord downs his shot of vodka and chases it quickly with half the pint of beer. He looks over at the happy couple, and they are looking at him. The woman waves and smiles as they leave the bar. Chord displays a grandiose smile and returns a farewell wave. *Happiness is camouflage for despair.*

When the door closes behind the woman and her male friend, Chord downs the rest of his beer and orders another shot.

The streets are darker than usual, cold and empty. Chord is a prisoner in this city, enclosed in concrete and bricks, tormented by memories. The city is a battlefield of walking casualties—mindless shells of men lying in their own filth. Once they were young and maybe even happy. Now they cling to the street the way broken ornaments cling to a disposed-of Christmas tree after New Year's Day.

The only drunk stumbling around tonight is Chord.

The walls are painted. The graffiti reminds Chord of the bar bathroom and the beautiful woman. He enters a small bodega to buy a pack of gum. In the back corner of the store, Chord notices cans of spray paint watching him from the top shelf.

Chord stands in front of a wall of brick covered in graffiti. It's a dark corner of the city illuminated only by the apartment lights surrounding the area. Chord glances back and forth to see if anyone is around. Then he begins to spray-paint over the graffiti. A large *H*. Then an *A*. As he finishes a large *S*, he hears footsteps behind him. A sharp pain brings Chord to his knees, and he hears angry voices.

One says, "Yo, mothafucka! Who do you think you are? You fuckin' crazy?"

Chord tries to speak, but the pain only allows a groan. He turns, and the last thing he sees is a foot heading toward him in slow motion, as if a plane is coming in for a landing on his face.

Chord's body goes limp, and two males continue to kick and stomp on him. After a few seconds of assault, one male spits on Chord, and the other, with Chord's paint, spray-paints Chord's limp body.

The two males walk away and enter one of the apartment buildings overlooking the wall.

Barely illuminated by the light from the apartment buildings, Chord lies on the sidewalk with a total loss of possibility, hope, belief, and bladder, as evidenced by a warm, clinging pant leg. A total loss of pride. He lies there in the fetal position, reborn, covered in his own bodily fluids, whimpering, cold, scared, and alone. A broken heart mends, but will a broken spirit? The only words Chord was able to spray before being attacked hover over his beaten body like the title over a piece of museum art: "Happiness is."

Manny and Eloise fold clothes and neatly stack them on tables at the clothing store. As they finish one table, they move on to the next. As they move on, a customer approaches the neatly folded stack and pulls it apart to find his size. He lifts it to his body, looks down at it, and then slovenly folds it and throws it down onto the pile. *Job security*, Manny thinks. *A revolving door of straightening things out and messing them up.*

Manny smiles and watches Eloise fold and laugh as they converse. Every time she looks up and sees him watching her, she pretends she doesn't. He notices the way her fingers tuck under the fold and gently pull and flip, her chipped nail polish and short fingernails, and the way one corner of her mouth curls up higher than the other when she smiles. One of her front teeth is slightly turned off course. It's subtle but unique. Manny can't help but soak her in.

Chord has a recurring dream that haunts him. He's crawling through what appears to be a giant hamster maze made of bright, transparent orange and green tubes of plastic, only he can't see through the plastic. The ground is lined with sand. He keeps crawling, searching for a way out, making lefts and rights, squeezing through parts of the maze that are almost full of sand.

Chord feels as if his oxygen is running out. He gasps for air. The more he crawls, the more it seems the plastic tunnels fill with sand. There's less and less room to maneuver, and he ends up flat on his belly, squirming around the maze. Then he's stuck, no longer able to move. The pressure of the rising sand squeezing him against the orange plastic tube becomes unbearable. He struggles to breathe. Finally, as he succumbs to suffocation, Chord wakes up.

This is the dream Chord has before he wakes up in the hospital bed.

Chord's parents stand when they see his eye open. Chord's face is mangled. His left eyelid is a blue bubble that has swollen over the rest of his eye. His bottom lip has a few visible stitches. One of his front teeth is chipped. His right hand is secured in a hard cast due to two broken fingers and a broken wrist. It looks as if a map of the world has been painted around his torso in black and blue. He focuses on his parents with his bloodshot right eye. A teardrop formulates and falls to his chest. "Why did you give up the guitar? I don't want to be like you. I don't want to settle for a life I don't want."

Chord's mother's eyes become watery. His father's demeanor changes.

Chord continues. "I don't want to settle because I'm afraid of failure."

Chord's father, fighting a lump of emotion in his throat, responds, "I did the best I could to give you a good life. I'm sorry if it wasn't enough. I'll be outside." He leaves the room.

"Your father and I have never discouraged you. We've never stopped you from doing what you've wanted. Have we?" Chord's mother asks.

"No," responds Chord. "But you never said I could do it either."

"Well, what is it you want to do?" exclaims his mother with slight frustration.

Chord stares at her with his bloodshot eye. A liquid trail streams from the corner of his eye. Snot gathers at his upper lip. He can't answer. He sits silently, just staring at his mother.

"Well, I can't help you if you can't help yourself. You should apologize to your father. We'll be back to pick you up tomorrow. Get some rest."

His mother exits, and Chord stares off at his reflection in the window. *Transparent. Pathetic. When you realize your worst enemy is yourself, hope becomes a threat.*

Chord's father pulls the car around to the hospital entrance. Chord's mother exits the hospital and gets into the passenger side.

"He's right, ya know." Chord's father looks at his wife. "He's right. I gave up."

Chord's mother says, "If supporting a family and working a tough profession to its completion is giving up, then what does that say about my life? We all sacrificed one thing for another. That's life."

"I love you. You raised our child and never judged me. You're a good woman, a wonderful mother, and the best wife any man could dream to have." Chord's parents embrace over the center console of their car. "I'm gonna play you a little melody when we get home." They kiss, and Chord's father drives away.

With a smile, Chord's mother exclaims, "I didn't know you still had that old guitar!"

Samantha sits with her friend Jessica in a restaurant on the Lower West Side of the city. The restaurant is small, with only four tables and a bar with five stools. A white tin ceiling complements the plush pink chair cushions. The place has a vintage-modern feel. Jessica is a tiny young woman in her midtwenties with straight black hair and high cheekbones. Her lips are artificially plump, and her accessories are well labeled.

"So how did it go? Tell me everything!" Jessica is way too enthusiastic.

"Well, he was—"

"Gorgeous and successful!" Jessica says, interrupting.

"Yes, he was a good-looking man. I mean, it was late, so we—"

"Yeah, why do you do that? I mean, go out at a normal time. This guy is a catch! Good looking, rich, and polite." Jessica laughs.

"I don't care about those things. I just want a guy who cares about me. I mean, all this guy wanted to do was snort blow and get me into his room." Samantha waves her hand to order another Bloody Mary.

"Oh hey, look at you. It's only eleven thirty." Jessica pushes out a laugh. "I mean, I would totally be with you, but I don't really have the funds."

"Really, Jess. You know I will take care of it." It's not uncommon for Samantha to take the bill. "It's funny. I met some guy in the bar briefly before Tom came in." She smiles.

"Shut up! Some bar guy caught your eye over Tom?"

"You shut up!" Samantha giggles. "There was something about him. I don't know."

"That's the poet in you. There is no love at first sight, and there is no good man in a bar at midnight!"

"I guess."

"Look, honey, you can't just be with any random joe in a bar. You're like royalty. You have to meet someone who can at least come close to your wealth. Some middle-class guy won't know what to do with you."

Samantha looks at Jessica with frustrated sadness in her eyes. "A good person is a good person. I'm just a trust-fund baby. I didn't earn anything."

Jessica seems to know not to push the issue. "Okay. I just want the best for you."

Chord awakens to the screaming of a teapot that can't take any more pressure. He's lying in his own bed. The swelling of his eye has subsided, allowing for vision. The stitches have been removed from his lip. He slowly leans across his bed, reaching for a medicine vial on his nightstand. He winces from a subtle pain that still resides in his torso. With a shake, two little white pills fall into his hand. Chord drops them into his mouth, and with a sip of water from a cup at his bedside, they make their descent into his bloodstream—little white soldiers at war with pain.

The war has been going on for about two weeks. He has been lying in his bed on house arrest, trapped. His profession doesn't allow its employees to leave their permanent residences when out sick. It's torture.

There's a knock at the door, and Chord's mother calls from the opposite side, "I made you tea! Can I come in?"

"Yes."

Chord's mother enters. "How are you feeling?"

"Fine." Chord wants to say that his bruised, scarred, broken body complements his bruised heart, broken spirit, and scarred youth. *But what would it matter?* he thinks. *I'm just a whiner.*

"Well, are you still in pain? Have you heard your father? He's playing and writing music again."

On the inside, Chord smiles. *My self-destruction. It's sad how some failures can be camouflaged by a false happiness. Our sad denials.* He responds aloud, "That's great."

"Yes, it is. Maybe what you said in the hospital was mean, but maybe it was necessary." The old necessary evil: necessities.

The waiting room is bland and stale. There are paintings of trees and the ocean, which create a grounding atmosphere. Chord sits on an old leather couch—probably donated. Chord's mother suggested he speak with a therapist. In light of the recent events, she thinks it will be a healthy option. Chord searched online for shrinks who carry his insurance and found this doctor—best of the worst.

"Mr. Samson?"

"Yes."

"Please come in." A little old man stands beside the open room door, gesturing for Chord to walk that way.

Chord sits in a leather chair with wooden legs. There's a clock on the wall behind him, and the therapist sits in front of him. The room is barren.

The therapist begins. "As you know, I'm Dr. Barkney. So what brings you here?"

"I've been feeling rather self-destructive lately." Chord doesn't break eye contact with the therapist.

"Okay. What do you believe is the cause of this destructive feeling?"

"I don't know, Doc. I bought a car when I got my job. The bill payments are high."

"So you feel financial strain?"

"Yes." Chord breaks eye contact and looks at his hands. He is squeezing the tip of his thumb. "You know, I just feel like I'm climbing this ladder to get to new heights, but I don't know where the ladder came from. Well, I do, but I just started climbing, and now I can't stop."

"Where did the ladder come from?"

"I'm a cop. My dad was a cop. He's been building this ladder for me my whole life."

"You don't want to be a cop?"

"I don't know. I mean, it's kind of cool. I just want to do something for me."

"Well, what is it you want to do? You are young. You don't have to stay in a job that makes you unhappy."

"Yeah. I have all these bills now." Chord pauses. He looks at the therapist as if to wait for the next question.

"What would you like to do as a profession? Or even a hobby?"

"I don't even know. I think I'm going crazy."

"What makes you think you are going crazy?"

"Well, I've been seeing things. Like people from work." Chord turns and looks at the clock.

"As in dating someone from work? Don't worry about the time."

"I just feel sad all the time. Not like suicidal!" Chord chuckles at the thought. "Just unhappy."

"Well, is the person from work making you feel unhappy?"

"No. Yes. Not really. I feel like my unhappiness is making me see the people." Chord smiles a hopeless smile. "That makes no sense. I know."

"Look, Chord, don't worry about making sense. Don't worry about what I'm thinking about you. Don't worry about the time. Just tell me what's bothering you. Talk. If you're holding on to anything negative—resentment or unhappiness—just talk to me. You deserve to be happy. And my goal is to make you realize that or, if you know that already, to feel it."

"I just feel sad and angry. I feel like my father's failures made him stop me from trying to be anything but secure. I feel like I was pushed so hard to fear everything with the slightest chance for failure that I can't even attempt to try! And I did something, and it made me feel—" Chord stops and looks back up at the therapist. "It made me feel something."

"What kind of something?"

"Like my boundaries aren't real." Chord thinks about the woman in the bar with the warm smile and blue eyes.

"We form ideas in our heads. Sometimes they can be modified or even planted there by our friends and family. Then we let those ideas run our daily life. We let those thoughts of how we should be or should act hinder our potential. You're not perfect, Chord. You will make mistakes. You will make attempts and fail. Don't let that fear of messing up drive you."

Manny sits across from Eloise; they are both unpacking clothes from boxes. Manny is in his glory. They are giggling and chatting, seemingly the perfect couple. Manny stops working. It's as if he's summoning all the power in the universe and within him to finally let go of his deepest secret. "I have something to tell you. Well, ask you," he says.

Eloise looks up from unpacking and waits.

"I don't think you should go through with marrying your fiancé."

"What?"

"Well, I know he's a good man, but I just … I think that you and I … I mean, I feel like there is something here."

"What? Where? What are you talking about, Manny? I love Jason."

"Well, what about what we have? I mean, I feel like … I mean, don't you love me? I love you."

Eloise puts her hand on Manny's cheek. "Manny, we are great friends. I care about you as a friend. I would never want to see anything bad happen to you, and I want you to be happy, but that's all. I love Jason, and I'm excited to marry him."

Manny stares into the box in front of him. He can't lift his head. "I'm sorry." He gets up and, without looking at Eloise, leaves the store.

"Manny, wait!" Eloise calls out to him, but she doesn't try to stop him. She sits in awe and confusion.

Chord awakens and rolls over to look at his alarm clock. It's eleven o'clock at night. He rises from his bed and dresses. "I'm not going to be a prisoner of my bruises. I'm going to enhance my existence." He thinks of the woman in the bar.

Soon Chord pulls his car up to the front of his precinct and parks. When he walks in, the sergeant at the desk asks how he is. "Fine," he responds without missing a step to the locker room.

Chord opens his locker, takes out his handgun, conceals it in his jacket pocket, and exits the precinct with a quick wave.

Soon after, his car pulls into a parking spot on a dark city street. From under his driver's seat, he pulls out a small crowbar. He exits his car slowly to avoid sharp bites of pain in his ribs. He lets the crowbar drop into a pant leg, securing the hooked end in his belt. Chord walks a few blocks and enters a small bodega. Upon exiting, he's carrying a black plastic bag holding two cylindrical objects.

Chord stands in front of a brick wall covered in graffiti, illuminated only by the lights of the occupied apartments in the buildings surrounding him. On the wall in front of him are the words *Happiness is*, partially covered by other graffiti. Chord whistles the "Whistle While You Work" melody as loudly as he can while pulling a spray-paint can from his black plastic bag. He begins to spray the wall, whistling while he works—first a capital *F*. When Chord finishes spraying his message, he takes a few steps back from the wall to view his art. From behind, he hears two voices. Chord smiles.

One says, "This bitch must be fuckin' crazy, bro!"

The other man replies, "Isn't this that fool we jacked up a few weeks ago?"

Chord turns with his gun outstretched in front of him. Behind him, in giant red letters, is a message of disaster. A big "Fuck you" is painted on the wall. It hovers over Chord as he aims his gun. The two men throw their hands to the sky and plead to be saved. They apologize. They whimper.

With a smile, Chord screams, "Get your asses on the ground! Now! I want you both on your stomachs!" They beg, apologize, whine, and sniffle. They comply. "You parasites! You fucking tough-guy pussies! What'd you think? You think these are your streets? Fuck you! I work hard!"

"Please, bro, don't do this!" one man says.

"I work fucking hard! My life isn't easy! I need help sometimes! I need release! I work and work and work. I have bills! I see my parents. I see them giving up everything! For me!"

"Oh God, please!"

"God? God's not gonna help you, scumbags! You're trash! My parents worked at supporting and raising me, and I blame them for my cowardice. No more!"

The two men lie on their stomachs, whimpering and pleading. Snot runs from their noses.

Chord rants over them, flailing his gun. The teapot whistles. Chord reaches into his pants and pulls out the crowbar. Chord's eyes well with fear and rage, and he quietly exclaims, "No more! I'm taking charge of my life." He raises the crowbar over his head.

After a few wild swings, there's no more whimpering. No screaming. No begging. No pleading. There's only a quiet "Fuck you."

—2—

Chord enters the bar and takes his seat in the back corner. It waits for him there. He orders a Jack Daniels on the rocks, his eyes distant. A slight hint of fear and excitement hovers around him. He tilts his head back and rests the edge of his glass on his lip, swallowing peace. Swallowing his nerves. Swallowing his anger. Swallowing his fear. Swallowing his whiskey.

He levels off with the glass half empty, and then there's a tap on his shoulder. Chord jumps almost out of his seat as he turns. There before him, better than any drink, is the blue-eyed woman.

"Why are you in my seat again?" she asks with a flirtatious tone. "And what the hell happened to your face?"

Chord just stares at her, happy to see her and not a group of gangbangers ready to kill him.

"Cat got your tongue?"

"No. I just didn't expect to see you again."

"Well, you're in my bar." She smiles widely and warmly. It's funny how sometimes a smile can give a person hope.

"I didn't know you owned this bar."

"I don't, silly. I see you enjoy frequenting it."

"Yeah. It, uh, comforts me." Chord smiles.

"Well, what happened to your face?"

Chord has almost forgotten his face is noticeably beaten. "Actually, I was jumped that night we met."

Her mouth drops open. "No way! Who did it? Are you okay?"

Chord smiles at her concern and thinks, *I wish this girl could love me. She's wonderful.* He responds, "Just some guys. Guess they didn't like me in their neighborhood."

"Jeez. That's horrible."

"Yeah. Well, I'm sure it won't happen again." There's a quiet moment as they both stare deep into each other's eyes. "So are you meeting your boyfriend again? Man, what time is it anyway?"

"I don't have a boyfriend. And it's about midnight or a little after."

"What about the guy you left with last time?"

"Well, aren't you Curious George? That was a month ago."

Something in Chord has changed, as though his actions have pushed him past some invisible confidence barrier—a metamorphosis of sorts.

Chord answers honestly from the heart, not like the usual part he plays for the audience. "I just find you soothing to be around."

She giggles. "That's definitely a new one."

"So then you're just here for a drink?"

"No, actually—this is embarrassing."

They pause, and Chord smiles.

She says, "Ugh! I'm on an internet dating site. It's hard

to meet people, and I meet them here just in case they are wacky. If so, I can sneak out the back door."

"Oh. That's not embarrassing. Why don't we go grab a late-night snack?"

"Hello! I'm waiting for someone."

"Who cares? Whoever walks in that door doesn't know you as well as I do now. We have history."

"Ha! I don't even know your name!"

"Chord."

"And besides, I don't know if I want to go out with some barfly who's always drinking alone on weeknights and picking fights."

"That makes perfect sense then. Meet a guy from the internet at midnight in a bar." Chord smiles.

"Anyway, what kind of name is Chord?"

"What's your name?"

"Samantha."

"Well, it's nice to meet you, Samantha. My name is Chord, and I'm a newly functioning alcoholic."

Samantha laughs.

"So what do ya say we get outta here and grab a bite? We'll go somewhere with a back door."

Chord awakens in his bed. The clock tells him it's ten o'clock in the morning. He winces as he rolls onto his back. He shakes awake two white soldiers and swallows them. He lies back. A new sense of calm whispers in his ear. A smirk long forgotten by the muscles in his face reintroduces itself. There is something about a woman's attention that brightens the day, and Chord likes it.

Chord sits at the breakfast table. His mother cooks at

the stove. His father reads the newspaper. "I'm sorry about what I said in the hospital," Chord says.

His father looks up from the paper and nods with recognition, as if to say, "Not a problem. Life goes on."

Chord's mother smiles to herself.

Words, gestures, communication—simple in their complexity yet profound.

"You know you can get into trouble by going out when you're supposed to be home sick," his dad says.

"I know. I just felt a little stir crazy. And I met someo—"

"Well, most likely, no one will come around in the middle of the night, but ya never know." Chord's father looks back down at his paper.

"I know, Dad."

Chord's mother steps in, begins to place the food on the table, and asks Chord to continue what he was about to say. "Never mind," he says.

Talking to parents should be easy. Unfortunately, it's not. Chord thinks back to when he and Manny would talk about the things they couldn't discuss with others. Friendship is strange that way. When Manny and Chord were children in elementary school, Manny was a funny-looking kid and always quiet. One morning, the class bully cornered Manny and went to town sucker-punching him. Everyone laughed. It was the laughter people laugh when thanking God it's not them. Kids don't know any better.

After that incident, Manny shut down. He didn't say a word the whole day. Then, after school, Chord and Manny walked to Manny's house. Manny's father asked how his day was, and Manny just screamed, "Don't talk to me!"

Later, when Chord and Manny were alone in his room,

Manny told Chord how embarrassed he was. Chord didn't know what to do, so he just put his hand on Manny's shoulder, and they sat quietly for a moment. Then they played video games as if nothing had ever happened.

Sometimes adults don't know any better either.

Samantha sits alone in a coffee shop, staring off into some other world. She stares blankly at her laptop screen, away. She's surrounded by lone patrons writing, reading, typing, and talking on cell phones, connected by disconnection.

Samantha comes back from wherever she was lost and swipes her finger across the mouse pad of her laptop. The screen is revived. On it is a poem. Sometimes words can be people's extension. She reads it to herself in an almost audible whisper:

> Stare across an open plain.
> Contact never made.
> Through gazing eyes,
> your body language displays a Closed sign.
> A curiosity never to be discovered,
> shattered by the awkward smile of another.

She sighs. "Such crap." She looks up at a couple sitting together—all their smiles and giggles. *Sometimes we condemn ourselves to loneliness.*

Samantha thinks of Chord and the food they shared last night. She receives a message on her laptop from the dating site. She closes out the message without even reading it and smiles. She packs up her laptop, cleans her table, and leaves the coffee shop.

A small black-and-gray cat purrs and moans at the edge of the bed. Animals express compassion and tolerance. They wait patiently. They love unconditionally, unafraid to display their need of someone else. What kind of animals are humans then? They're scared of life, emotion, and change. They're scared to give themselves completely to another, to accept love, and to follow their instincts.

The cat stares at a doorknob. The knob begins to jiggle. Then there's the sound of a key opening the lock, and the door opens. Samantha enters and swoops her cat up into her arms. The cat purrs and meows. Samantha kisses its head. "Hey, buddy! How was your day? Were you waiting here all day for me?" She puts the cat down and closes the apartment door. She's in her cubicle world.

She walks toward the food bowl on the floor at the end of the bed and empties some cat food into it. Her apartment is condensed into a space about twenty feet wide and fifty feet long. It's a glorified cell.

She walks about the apartment, picking up clothes from the floor, cleaning the dishes in the sink, and pushing down the garbage in the pail to achieve more space. Eventually, she showers and then lies down with some leftover food and her cat. At about nine o'clock, in front of the television, she falls asleep.

Samantha awakens to the generic ringtone of her cell phone. She answers.

"Hey, Samantha. It's Chord."

Still groggy from being woken up, Samantha responds, "Chord?"

"Yeah. The really wacky alcoholic who wouldn't let you escape out the back door of your bar."

"Oh, I thought you were the other guy I know named Chord," she says, and Chord chuckles. "You know what time it is?"

"Yeah, about eleven o'clock, I think. I was wondering if you wanted to get a drink."

Samantha smiles. "Chord, it's the middle of the night."

"Yes, it is."

"Well, I was sleeping."

"Oh. I'm sorry. Now that you've woken up, you wanna get something to drink?"

"Chord, I don't know if I can start a relationship with an alcoholic."

"Well, I'm not only an alcoholic."

Samantha giggles. "Seriously, do you drink every night?"

"No. I'm just going through something. I'm on house arrest until I get better, but my job won't call in the middle of the night, so it's my only time to sneak away."

"Well, I don't kn—"

Chord interrupts. "Listen, I'm heading over to the bar now. If you meet me there, great. If not, I'll stalk you at a more reasonable hour next time. Deal?"

"You've got yourself a deal, mister." Samantha ends the call, rolls onto her back, smiles, and sighs.

As Chord parks his car across from the bar, his phone rings. He excitedly fishes it from his pocket, thinking it could be Samantha. Manny's name is illuminated on the screen. Just before disappointment can set in, out of the corner of his eye, Chord sees Samantha enter the bar. He smiles and ignores the call. *He'll understand. The courting process can be demanding on a man's time.*

Chord walks across the street and enters the bar. Samantha greets him with a generous smile.

"I can't believe I'm here right now." Samantha smirks and looks excited.

"Well, I'm glad you came." Chord stares at her with a confident contentment.

"How are you feeling?"

Chord's smile widens. "All good things when I'm around you."

Samantha looks down at her feet and smiles. They find seats at the bar and order drinks.

"So what do you do that has you up all hours of the night?" Samantha looks up at him. Her eyes carry an innocent curiosity.

Chord processes the question as though he is afraid to tell the truth, but he doesn't want to lie. "I'm a police officer."

"Oh my God, no way! I would've never suspected that! That's so cool." Samantha smiles and seems to let herself relax into the chair.

Chord is perplexed. It's as if she's relieved.

"So did you always want to be a cop? That's so cool. I mean, I think I've used the word *cool* more times in this moment than I have since I was five years old." She smiles with a hint of embarrassment.

Chord smiles, slightly in disbelief. "I never wanted to be a cop, actually. Sorry to disappoint you." He lifts his hands palm up and shrugs.

"Oh, okay. What made you decide to become one then?"

"It runs in the family." Chord looks into her eyes to see

the disapproval, but it's not there. "I mean, I like aspects of it."

"Well, what did you want to do? Or I mean, what do you want to do?"

"I'm not really sure. I enjoy writing but don't do much of it." Chord begins to feel insecurity creeping into mind and body. He shifts in his seat and looks down at the ground to avoid Samantha's eyes.

"That's pretty amazing. I write too! I mean, not professionally. I dabble." She smiles. The same creature seems to sneak its way into her.

We cannot let insecurity motivate our thoughts and actions. "What do you do?" Chord asks.

Samantha now looks down at the ground and shifts in her seat. "You mean other than internet dating and writing poetry in coffee shops?"

"Yes. Please don't tell me you make a living by internet dating."

"Um, no. I actually inherited money. So I basically just exist."

Chord isn't sure what to ask next. He doesn't want to be rude, and he can see that this topic is making Samantha uncomfortable. "I want to know you—all about you—but if you aren't in the mood to share right now, that's fine."

Samantha can't remember the last time she had a genuine conversation with a man or at least with a man who knew he had flaws. "My parents died when I was young. My father was the founder and president of Allman Securities. You know, it's funny because people usually don't have any problem saying how lucky I am now, but they never think about the price of my life."

"I'm sorry."

"Oh God, please don't be." Samantha smirks, her eyes calm. "I don't get a chance to talk about it much. Or maybe I don't usually care to."

After a couple more drinks, Samantha looks at Chord as if she has something important to say. "I really need to get to sleep."

Chord smiles, "Okay." He motions to the bartender for the check.

"I really want to take you home with me." Samantha picks at her coaster, which is moist and soggy from the condensation of her drink and the wet bar. "But I don't want you to get the wrong idea." She pauses as if she is the second-to-last contestant in a spelling bee and has just been given a difficult word.

"I want to be where you are. I'm in no rush," Chord says.

All is black and silent. Chord opens his eyes to find a small black-and-gray cat standing on his chest and looking down at him. Chord smiles.

"Hey, hey, hey, little buddy! He's mine." Samantha pulls the cat from Chord's chest.

"Don't get jealous. The cat likes me!"

"Of course the cat likes you. I invited you in." Samantha rolls on top of Chord, looks at him as though she's going to tell him a secret, and then kisses him.

In his mind, Chord reflects on his feelings for Heather and how he thought he loved her. *Is love real or just a word?* Samantha's mouth is perfect. *Is it that easy to bounce from one love to another? Samantha is different.* It's as though Chord has known her his whole life. The level of comfort he feels when he's around her is astonishing. *Sometimes our fear of hopes and desires that seem out of reach can be even more frightening when they seem attainable.*

Chord pulls away from Samantha. "I should get going. Never know when my job might decide to check up on me." He is already dressed because they both passed out on Samantha's couch while watching television. He stands up, leans down, and kisses Samantha.

Samantha grabs Chord by the shirt. "Thanks for being so sweet and not pushing. Thanks for being refreshing."

As he leaves the apartment, he can't help but wonder if all the guys she meets end up there, serenaded by those same words.

Chord's father looks up from his paper as Chord enters the kitchen. "I really think you're pushing your luck. If you get suspended without pay, how are you going to pay your bills?"

"Dad, they aren't going to be looking for me in the middle of the night. And good morning to you too."

"What if they'd called this morning? It's ten o'clock."

"I dunno. I really don't care. This job is bullshit anyway."

"Bullshit. I've been getting a pension without working for years. I don't have to worry about getting sick, and I'm doing what I love."

"Thanks to me."

"What's that supposed to mean?"

Chord's mother intervenes. "Chord, that's enough! Sit down, and have some breakfast."

Chord sits, and his mother places the food on the table and pours Chord a cup of coffee. They all begin eating. "Oh yeah, Manny called in the middle of the night," his mom tells him. "He sounded drunk. I think you should stop drinking so much."

"I'm not an alcoholic, Mom. I wasn't with him anyway."

"Where were you then? You've been going out every night."

"I met someone."

Chord's mother smiles. Even his father seems interested. "Go on," she says.

"Nothing. That's all. I just met someone."

Chord's father asks with a comical tone, "Man or woman?"

"Oh, shut up!" responds Chord's mother.

Chord smiles. "A woman. Unless Samantha has a penis." Chord and his father chuckle.

"That's gross!" Chord's mother slaps his arm and begins giggling too.

Chord enters his room. It's a mess. *It's funny how when your mind is a mess, it reflects in the things around you.* He plucks his dirty clothes from the floor and collects the empty beer bottles. He straightens out his bed and reorganizes his desktop.

Chord's cell phone rings. "Hello?"

It's Samantha. "Hi. I know you just left. I just wanted to say I had a lot of fun last night. Even if all we did was fall asleep to the TV."

"So did I." Chord smiles. He scans his room, appreciating the cleanliness of it.

Samantha smiles at Chord while he drives. Her smile melts away the rest of the world. Chord looks at her in disbelief that this woman is sitting in his car and smiling at him. Her beauty is overwhelming.

"What are you looking at?" she asks.

"You."

"What are you thinking about?"

"You. Naked."

Samantha smacks Chord's arm. "Creep! And I thought you had more depth." She pauses. "But maybe if we survive this." She smiles innocently.

"Yeah, I guess I let you wait long enough." He smiles. "No, really, what I'm thinking. I'm thinking about how lucky I am. I'm trying to figure out whether or not you're real."

"Well, we've been seeing each other for about two weeks now. So that would make this the longest dream ever! Or you're a complete nut."

Chord suggestively smiles. "Yeah, I was thinking nut too."

Samantha leans over and kisses Chord. She kisses his neck and ear.

"Ow!"

Samantha bites Chord's ear.

Chord chuckles. "What was that for?"

"I wanted to make sure you weren't dreaming." They kiss. Chord swerves.

A few minutes later, the car pulls into a dirt parking lot next to a small runway. At the end of the runway waits a Cessna 208.

"I can't believe we're doing this." Chord opens his eyes wide and smiles.

"Oh my God, neither can I."

Chord and Samantha sit through a short lesson on how to arch properly when leaving the plane. They can't take their eyes off each other. Samantha sits in between Chord's legs and lays her head back on his chest. There is nervous energy, excitement, and life pumping through their veins.

How can a connection feel so strong when it hasn't existed for even a month? Chord remembers this feeling with Heather too, and it scares him. But Samantha is so real. Chord smells her hair. He feels his heart beating hard and fast and wonders if Samantha can feel it.

Chord's phone vibrates. It's Manny. He ignores it and falls back into the moment.

Chord sits across from Samantha as the plane rumbles, shimmies, and lifts off from the ground—like love. Their eyes speak to each other, speaking of fear and happiness and the unknown experience to follow.

At thirteen thousand feet, the door is opened. It's real now. Samantha locks onto her tandem instructor. Chord wonders if Samantha is still meeting people online. They inch forward toward the door. Chord locks onto his instructor. Samantha's at the edge of the door now, rocking. One. Two. "I'll see you on the ground." Three, and she's gone.

Chord inches toward the door. At the edge, the world below appears surreal. The wind rushes through his soul. He is rocking. One. *Can love be real?* Two. *Samantha is real.* Three. Chord is scared. *Gravity—hell of a force. You don't feel like you're falling. There is room for anything in your mind except the sensation.*

It's peaceful.

The cat runs to the door. Samantha pushes the door open with her backside as she and Chord embrace, kissing each other. They almost fall into the room. The cat dodges their feet. They drop their bags where they stand. A picture of them smiling after landing from the skydive looks up at them.

Their mouths are open as their tongues dance. Their hands caress each other's body. Chord slides his hand up Samantha's shirt and grabs her breast. Samantha slides her hand down the front of Chord's pants and gently strokes his penis. The cat meows. They fall onto the bed. Samantha rolls on top of Chord and sits up. She pulls her shirt and bra over her head. Her body is smooth. Her nipples are erect. She looks at Chord with her blue eyes. She hopes he can't see fear in them.

She waits for just a moment to let Chord view her naked breasts. Then she reaches down and unhooks his belt and pants. As they kiss, Chord wiggles his pants off of his ankles. He kisses her neck and slides his mouth down to her breast. He fills his mouth with her. He turns her onto her back and gently releases her breast from his mouth. He pulls his shirt over his head, and their naked bodies touch for the first time.

It's as if their bodies become one—the warmth and sweat and saliva. Chord slides his mouth down to her stomach. He pulls her pants off and slides off his underwear. The cat watches for a moment as their bodies entwine, moving up and down, and then goes to the other room and curls up on the couch. Manny's name illuminates as Chord's phone vibrates on the floor.

Chord's mother sits at the breakfast table. "So what's going on?"

"What do you mean?" Chord asks.

"There is something going on with you. It seems to be a good thing, but you don't talk to us anymore."

"I've been seeing that girl. Samantha."

"That's fantastic. How long has it been?" Chord's father looks up from his paper.

"About three weeks. We went skydiving together. It was amazing."

"You did what?" his mother says. "That's dangerous."

Chord's dad puts his paper down. "Was it expensive?"

"It was an amazing experience."

"So where does Samantha live, and when do we get to meet her?" his mother asks.

"I dunno, Mom. I mean, it hasn't been that long. I don't want to scare her away just yet." Chord smiles.

Chord's father picks his paper up and begins reading again.

Chord's mother can see the excitement in Chord, even though he tries to hide it. "And where does she live?"

"In the city."

"Sounds expensive." Chord's father doesn't look away from his paper.

"You're probably right, Dad. Why would she want to settle with just a cop? She's probably out looking for a nice banker or high-paid musician as we speak."

"That's enough!" Chord's mother glares at her husband.

"Well, I'm going to take a nap. Fun's over; I have work tonight."

Chord lies on his back, looking up at the ceiling in his room, thinking, *There are so many options in this city. In this world.*

Why would she settle for me, when she could clearly have so much more? Chord thinks about the man in the suit the first night he met Samantha.

Samantha smiles as she sits in front of her laptop at the café, sipping on a coffee. She types,

> I love seeing you here
> in my heart,
> my mind.
> I'm not afraid of this fear,
> this romantic start,
> this rhyme.
> It's your embrace that has taken me closer
> to grace.
> Filled with joy now where emptiness
> lingered.

Samantha looks up and out the window at the people racing to get somewhere quickly. She thinks, *We are all in such a hurry to get somewhere that we miss the fact that we are even here.*

A woman stops on the sidewalk in Samantha's line of sight. She's about the same age. She looks as though she's been sleeping in the street. Her hair is dark and matted. Her eyes are bloodshot. Samantha slightly jumps when she sees the woman. The woman smiles at her with dirty teeth, almost as if taunting Samantha. It is as though there is history between them.

Samantha's eyes fill with sadness. The woman gives Samantha the finger, punches the glass window, and storms off.

—3—

Samantha hears her father screaming in the library room of their country home. She's tucked under her plush down comforter in an enormous room. Her father's voice sounds far away, and the echo of it rumbles in from under her closed door. "I told you that you are not to be in this house or any home that I own! You will not destroy Samantha with your pathetic choices and wasted blessings!"

"Oh, your precious Samantha. You've already probably destroyed her, and you don't even know it yet!" a female voice says.

"Oh yes, Melissa, your mother and I are destroying you with such a luxurious life. All the cultural traveling experience, the Ivy League education just within grasp, and never wanting for anything!"

"There it is! All I want is my father's love! But that was never for sale or—"

Samantha's father's voice tears into Melissa's voice. "You don't dare try to blame me for your choices! I have worked relentlessly so you can have the best this world has to offer! You were able to earn scholarships on your own merit. That free will to study hard and apply it to your schoolwork is the same free will that turned you into a junkie! A cautionary tale for Samantha is all you will ever be!" His voice breaks with sorrow. "I have given you more than a year's time to steer back on course. Top therapists. The best rehabilitation facilities this country has to offer. So this will be the last time you and I interact."

Samantha's eyes are laden with moisture. She pulls the comforter up over her ears and closes her eyes, squeezing out the tears as if wringing a towel dry. Then there's nothing but silence.

Samantha opens her eyes, and standing over her bed is the women from outside the coffee shop window. Her eyeballs are as black as night. Blood runs from needle holes in the veins of her arms. She opens her mouth and breathes out yellow smoke.

Samantha jumps from her sleep. The cat jumps too at the foot of the bed. Her pillow is soaked in sweat, and her face is moist with tears cried. She breathes deeply and finds reality.

Stolsky's mouth hangs open as he snores. Chord's eyelids bounce open and slowly lower and then bounce open again. Drunken couples and singles stroll by the patrol car. The radio is quiet. Sitting across the street, huddled together against a building, staring at Chord, are the dead boy and old woman. Chord sees them, and they lock eyes.

Just then, Chord's phone vibrates with a text message from Samantha. He looks down at the phone, and the message reads, "Hey, baby! I'm going to sleep now. Muah!"

Chord smiles, and when he looks up, the dead boy and dead old woman are gone. *Trust is a funny thing.* Chord's face turns somber as his mind wanders. *Trusting a significant other is just like gambling. One woman cheats and lies after three years of a trusting relationship for no reason other than money. What can be said about a relationship three weeks in the making? Is that human nature? Are we all waiting for the better deal? Am I?*

Chord doesn't respond to the text. His insides tighten with fear and anxiety.

In life, there are moments that redefine who we are or reveal who we have always been. Our most frightening revelations. They come at different times, sometimes many and sometimes only one.

Chord stares at himself in his locker mirror. Displayed on his phone is the message from Samantha. He realizes the time of her text is about the same time she would normally be going out to meet someone. He thinks of her internet date the night they met. He begins to type a response text but stops. *Why would she settle for me? She could have anyone.* He sends no response.

Chord quietly ponders, *Is happiness camouflage for despair? Am I happy or distracted?* The inner turmoil Chord feels is palpable.

His moment of realization is interrupted by the reverberation of a fart throughout the locker room and the cackle of the other officers. The sound and the response to the sound burn Chord's brain, and as if touching hot metal, he flinches with fury and turns over his locker, spilling paperwork, handcuffs, and uniform pieces onto the ground in front of him. Angry at himself and the juvenile actions of his coworkers, he furiously shoves all the spilled possessions back into his turned-over locker, closes it, and locks it.

Heads peek around the aisle to see what the commotion is. Chord stands the locker upright and storms out of the locker room like a man possessed.

As Chord exits the precinct, still pissed off, and walks across the street, he sees his car in the light of the almost risen sun. It taunts him. In this moment of angst, Chord sees not just his car but the reason for all the problems in his world. It's why he must cope with the ignorance of coworkers and sleep throughout the day so he can wake in the night, and it reminds him of how immature his decision-making was and how he overextended his budget. He hears his dad's voice in his head, telling him not to take out loans and waste money on cars.

Sitting in the driver's seat is the dead boy, smiling. His mangled head is open and spilling gore. Chord runs toward his car and begins to repeatedly kick the passenger-side door. With each wild, flailing kick, Chord's foot leaves behind cavernous dents. The more Chord kicks, the more the dead boy laughs. His laughter is not that of a young teen but that of an old man full of knowledge, as if death matures those it chooses, enabling them to see the world with a more patient eye and more understanding and to pity the living, whose problems are so trivial.

"Yo, Chord! What the fuck are you doing?"

Chord is startled to find Stolsky behind him, observing his behavior. "I was—"

"Are you okay, man? Look at your car." Stolsky seems to truly care about Chord.

Chord has no words. He stares at his damaged car. He

feels his damaged ego and damaged soul. He doesn't look at Stolsky. He just raises his hand and delicately waves off his actions, hoping it will appear he is still in control. Then he gets in his car and drives off.

Where does the angst hide? The brutal anger? The resentment? It's hardest to cope when such feelings of despair are misunderstood. The car races down the interstate as unknowing of its destination as the madman behind its controls, misguided rage rocketing away from the rising sun.

Chord sucks in a deep breath and briefly holds it, as if to allow the oxygen to circulate through his body. A vibration from within his pocket indicates that someone is calling him. He reaches for his cell phone, and illuminated is Stolsky's name. "Of course he's calling. He must think I'm wacked out of my brain. Jesus, that must have looked psychotic." Chord ignores the call. "What am I going to do? I can't go back. I want to disappear."

Chord awakens in his car. The seat is back as far as it can go, allowing Chord to be almost prone. The sun is high in the sky. The car rests about a hundred feet from the road, on an open grassy field. Chord's face is shiny with a layer of oil and sweat from the humidity. A gentle, warm breeze brings with it the smell of freshly cut grass, and it reminds Chord of being young and lying on his front lawn while looking up at the sky and daydreaming of lives he would someday live.

Chord sits up and cranks his head around slowly to loosen the muscles in his neck. He imagines himself a boy out on the grassy field, and his eyes glisten with emotion. He looks at his phone and sees that he has several missed calls—not from Stolsky, as he would have thought, but from his mother. He dials to call his voice mail.

Another defining moment is about to jar loose the pattern of his behavior and maybe even alter his state of mind—the final shove that might send him over another edge. The voice mail was left by his mother.

"Chord, honey? I've been trying to reach you all day, and I keep getting your voice mail. I wanted to tell you this in person." There is a pause—the kind of pause that only bad news can follow. "Manny was found by his parents. Chord, honey, he killed himself. He's dead. I'm so sorry. Please call me as soon as you can."

Chord scrolls down the contact list on his cell phone to Manny's name. He presses the call button. His eyes glisten. The call goes straight to Manny's voice mail. "No! No! No! No! Answer the phone! Please!" Chords hits the send button again. He gets Manny's voice mail.

Chord chokes on his emotions. He tries to breathe. He dials his house number.

Chord's mother answers. "Chord?" Her voice is broken with sadness.

"Mom, he's really gone?"

"Chord, where are you?"

"Is he really gone?" he yells.

"Yes. He's gone. Come home, Chord. Where are—"

Chord interrupts. "How did he do it?"

"Chord, why don't you come—"

"Tell me!"

"They found him hanging."

Chord's eyes close, releasing tears down his red cheeks. He breathes deeply, as if to summon the strength to speak.

"I'll be home in a few days." He presses the end button and drops his phone into his lap.

His eyes are focused on some unknown, faraway point. There aren't any more tears. His cheeks are wet and red, and a small drip of snot slowly travels down toward his upper lip. He looks through his missed calls, and next to Manny's name is the number nine. Chord checks his voice mail list. There is a message from Manny from the previous night.

Chord presses the play button, and there is a slight pause. Then Manny's voice says, "Chord, I'm sorry I couldn't say these things to you in person. I just wasn't strong enough. Life is too hard, man. I am just so tired of waiting around for some fantastic change that makes my life better. Waiting around isn't gonna get anyone anywhere. It's up to us to change our lives by doing. The world will go on long after we are gone. Live, Chord. Do what I couldn't. Change your life. Survive. Take chances. Happiness is everywhere. I wish I'd found it. Thank you for being my friend. I'll see you on the other side."

Here it is—the undeniable end of innocence, the slipping away of youth's remembrance. Chord looks at himself in the rearview mirror. In the backseat, he sees the dead boy and woman. He isn't startled. He doesn't flinch or look away. He accepts them for that moment.

He hurls the car door open as if the car lacks oxygen. He stumbles out and falls to his knees in the grass. His fingers grab at the ground and sink into the grass and dirt, and he clenches his fists around the ground and pulls his head into the grass. In the darkness of his closed eyes, his mind reveals Manny and himself as children, running in a grassy field with wide smiles, pretending to be heroes impenetrable to negativity—smiles not yet marked by age and knowledge.

Chord rolls onto his side and then flat on his back, looking up at the sky. Tears once again begin their gentle descent down the sides of his face toward his ears.

Chord feels his heart beating at an unusually fast pace. He hears the muffled swish of beats deep in his ear canal. His hand raises his handgun slowly up and away from his lap. Chord watches it rise. Slowly, the muzzle changes direction. It lands at the base of Chord's chin.

With a flash, the strangest feeling rushes through Chord's body. It's not quite fear and not quite excitement. It's numbness. It's almost blissful. A strange warmth surrounds his teeth, and the taste of iron fills his mouth. Bubbled bursts splatter down onto his hand and gun. A steady red stream falls, splashing down onto his knees.

Chord sees himself in what appears to be a mirror, but his reflection doesn't match his movements. It's Chord but not Chord, laughing with delight. An air horn blasts in the distance. He smells grass and dirt and feels a cold shiver.

Chord awakens in the field, next to his car. The moon hovers overhead. "The gun!" Chord jumps up from the ground to search his car. All is still as he left it. He wraps the gun in a shirt from the backseat, places it on the roof of the car, and opens the trunk. Chord pulls a backpack from the trunk and places the wrapped gun in it. He leans into his car, picks a jacket up off the floor, and shoves it into the backpack.

Chord sets out on foot toward the road. The empty,

battered car watches as he walks off. His phone vibrates in the grass at the driver's side of the car, illuminating Samantha's name—an almost inaudible farewell.

Chord walks for almost an hour before a tractor trailer finally stops. It stands alone in the moonlight at the side of the empty road, spitting hydraulics and settling in a small cloud of dust. Chord jogs to close the distance. He climbs up onto the passenger side of the truck.

Behind the wheel, with his body cocked toward Chord, sits a middle-aged man. He looks like a creepy uncle who uncomfortably greets you with a big kiss. The single uncle who lacks physical attention from any woman.

The truck-driving uncle says his name is Stanley. He appears to be in his fifties. He has a round face with round features and an awkward smile, as if he hasn't spent time with another human for a long time. Creepy.

"Well, hop in if you are," Stanley says, and Chord opens the door, sits, and rests his backpack on his lap. "Don't know where it is you're going, but this road goes for at least another fifteen miles anyhow."

"Thank you for stopping."

"The good Lord works in mysterious ways." Stanley puts the truck in gear, and with a bounce, Chord begins moving toward uncertainty. "This here rig is Matthias. Helping spread the Lord's Word and ways."

"I'm Chord."

"Chord? Strange name."

"My dad was—is—a musician."

"Well, that adds up, don't it? What brings you out in the night on this long, empty road? Was that your vehicle broken down a few miles back?"

"Huh? My car? Oh yeah, it stalled out."

"So where are you heading?"

Chord attempts an awkward smile while trying to decide on an answer.

"The quiet type. On a spiritual journey and just don't know it yet maybe."

"I'm not very spiritual." Chord always gets a bad feeling about spiritual types. It's as if anyone who needs God in his or her daily life has screwed up somewhere and is hoping for some kind of salvation.

"Well, Chord, I understand that. We all need to find God in our own way. You don't have to share unless you want to. I'm drivin' down this road anyways."

"Thank you."

"Oh, I love this song!" Stanley cranks up the volume. How he even heard the song is a mystery to Chord. It was practically inaudible. Stanley cracks and squeaks along to the words in an attempt to mimic Bob Dylan: "'Broken dishes, broken parts. Streets are filled with broken hearts. Broken words never meant to be spoken. Everything is broken!' Wahoo! Sing it with me, Chord! 'Everything is broken!'"

As Chord sits watching, he loses control of the muscles in his face, and a smile forms. This Stanley might be crazy, but he is filled with some unusual happiness in company. Or maybe he sings like this to himself as well. Chord's body relaxes a bit as he lets himself enjoy the music, and the empty road seems to be a spectator—maybe not even as dreadful. Maybe, if just for that moment, it is a path to some new hope.

With a bang and shift, Chord wakes as the tractor trailer pulls off from the shoulder of a rest stop. The sun is beginning its rise from the horizon, the open land around is coated with a golden-orange hue, and the road glistens with moisture like a starry night sky.

"Well, good morning, friend! Gee whiz, you sure needed shut-eye."

Chord's eyes are still soaking up the beauty of the sunrise. "Yeah."

"He paints quite the picture, don't he?"

"He sure does, Stanley."

"Heck darn! So you aren't a heathen after all!"

"I lost my best friend. He was like my brother. He killed himself." The words fall out of Chords mouth as if they've been pressed up against the back of his lips, waiting. Chord feels a deep sadness. "I don't know what I am or what I believe in."

"I'm sorry, Chord." Stanley addresses the sky. "Please, Lord, have mercy on Chord's friend. Forgive him." Stanley looks down at his hands. One is folded over the other as they rest on the steering wheel. His eyes and demeanor go somewhere else, somewhere dark and secret. "Forgive us all our misdeeds." He looks back over to Chord. "You want to say a prayer?"

"No. Thank you, but no."

Chord is slightly frustrated with himself for falling on the shoulder of a stranger when in a personal crisis, especially a God-loving creepy-uncle truck driver. Chord is lost in thought. *Why is human interaction such a necessity?* Chord thinks about all the times he didn't answer Manny's calls. He wishes he had answered. He thinks maybe it would have made a difference.

The truck moves across the vast landscape toward the future, chasing the horizon like a dog chases its tail.

Chord and Stanley sit across from each other in an old diner booth. The rig is parked in the darkness of night alongside the diner. It's a rusty, dusty old diner that seems to have been exhumed from the past and brought back to life by a crank doctor. The outside lights are dull, if not broken, and inside, the fluorescent lights flicker and hum. The staff consist of an overweight woman in her midforties, a skeleton of a woman in her thirties, and an unhygienic gray-haired man who could be father, grandfather, or husband.

"So how did you arrive at the decision to devote your life to God?" Chord asks.

"Well, Chord, that there's a story."

"I'm not going anywhere in particular."

"I suppose you're not. The Lord saved me, see. I was in prison for kidnapping a seven-year-old girl." Stanley pauses and looks up at Chord as if for permission to stay seated.

"Go on."

"God found me lost and confused. He found me in the worst possible human condition. I can be forgiven. I sailed through the last few years of my purgatory. The love of the Lord saved me, and I'm so grateful to be saved. That truck is my home. My church. Here on the road, my sins and my urges are in the past." Stanley takes a breath. "I'm a good man. I can be forgiven." He pauses and looks out into the empty lot. Insects flutter and bounce into the window, searching for the light. The bright moon glares down. Stanley looks out the window as if he's looking at his demons. They're still out there, waiting.

Chord and Stanley order and eat without much conversation. Silence shared between two people can be profound in many ways—and awkward in many ways.

As the truck pulls away from the diner, an empty loneliness saturates the cab, and Chord feels it—some kind of unspeakable anger, disgust, and connection with Stanley. Maybe guilt. *We're all in it together. We all have been plagued. All connected in despair. Disdain.* Chord looks out at the passing world. The darkness. The star's dead light immortal to some universe. He thinks of his mother cooking at the stove and his father apologizing for being a great dad. Chord's eyes blur with salty emotion.

"What did you do with the little girl?" Chord asks.

"What?"

"The seven-year-old you kidnapped."

"Oh. She was beautiful. I wanted her. I wanted her so bad." As Stanley speaks, tears slowly make their way down his cheeks. It's as if his battle is still not over, as if his happiness is just camouflage. "She had the most youthful beauty. Her smile was so innocent. I pulled over and just lunged at her and her friends, and I grabbed her little waist and yanked her away from all of that innocence I admired. The screams excited me. Oh God!" Stanley begins to sob and speak through his cries. "That poor little angel!"

Chord shifts uncomfortably, as if Stanley's words are a brush, and the image of fear is painted in Chord's thoughts.

"I'm so sorry, Lord!" Stanley looks to the dark sky. "I didn't touch her! I didn't do those things in my mind!" He breathes and pauses and becomes emotionless. He redirects his attention to Chord. "I kept her in my van for about four days. Tied up and alone. I thought maybe I would kill myself."

Stanley pauses again and just stares out at the endless dark. "It would never be enough. If I had gone all the way, it would have never been enough. The high was so good. Her fear and my complete control. I returned her to her parents on the seventh day. I didn't touch her once, except the initial time I grabbed her and then holding her hand to walk her to her front door. But I destroyed her innocence. You see? I destroyed her life. It's our innocence that makes life wonderful and new. I'm a monster." He pauses again. "I'm a good man."

They both look out into the darkness toward the horizon. The headlights can illuminate only so far. Artificial light guides them.

The next day, they drive in silence, their personal lives shared. *Sometimes you can know people for years and not share any part of yourself, and then you meet someone, and a day later, you're crying on his shoulder.* Chord finds it ironic that he found a convicted kidnapper and pedophile to open up to. He thinks of Samantha. He can see her smile clearly in his mind and the way she looked at him with comfort and calm, the innocence common when starting out in a new relationship.

Stanley doesn't put the music on this day. He just stares straight ahead, deep in thought.

Stolsky enters a small room and takes a seat at a metal folding table. Across from him are two men in suits. The detectives call this room the Box. It's where they interview victims and perpetrators. Stolsky nods at the two men. "Tim. Jimmy."

Tim starts. "What's the deal with this partner of yours?"

"Tim, I don't even know this kid. I've worked with him for about a week or so. He stormed out of here all pissed off and started kicking the shit out of his car." Stolsky scoffs. "I mean, he went fucking nutty."

"Did he say anything during the nights or the days you worked with him?"

"No. He seemed like a nice kid. A little moody, but then again, who isn't when they first start midnights?"

The other detective, Jimmy, chimes in. "Well, we are getting stuck with this shit case until this kid shows up. Did he seem suicidal?"

"No. He seemed like every other cop. Tired and grumpy."

Tim says, "All right. Well, needless to say, if you hear from him, let us know." He stands up and pushes his hair back with both hands. "How's the family, Stols?"

"You know how it is. They keep me busy. Girls are getting big too fast."

"Oh Jesus, I her ya! Soon they'll be driving, and you'll be paying for college."

"Yeah, then you'll have another cop AWOL and another shitty case."

They all chuckle.

Chord and Stanley sit in a different booth at a different roadside diner in a different state with the same story. A family of three is sitting in the booth behind Stanley and

Chord: a mom, a dad, and a daughter about nine years old. Chord takes the last bite of food on his plate and excuses himself. He walks to the bathroom with a heavy feeling. A flood of doubt suddenly grabs hold of his chest and labors his breathing. He puts his hand to his head and thinks of his bills, his father, his car broken down and abandoned, his mother, and Manny, and he never even asked about Samantha's family. *I wish I had.*

Chord flicks on the bathroom light, and as if moving from the darkness to the light, he travels back to the bar's bathroom, where his scribbling on the door visually shouts, "Happiness is camouflage for despair"! With a panicky splash of cold water to his face, his eyes open to the diner bathroom he is presently in.

As he finishes eating, Stanley listens keenly to the little voice from behind him. The hairs on his arm stand erect. Microdroplets of perspiration form in the space between his chin and lower lip. He shifts in his seat. *Just a look. A peek*, he thinks to himself. His chest starts to rise and fall in quick succession. He can smell the cherry atop the sundae she's ordered.

Slowly, he turns, making it seem like a stretch. Her small shoulder is exposed in her little tank top. She has dirty-blonde hair. He makes eye contact with the parents. "Oh Lordy, I'm thinking I may just order myself a sundae!" he says with an overabundance of joy.

They smile, and the little girl giggles.

Stanley turns back around, and Chord is standing at the table. "Oh, hey buddy, you ready to go?"

"You're not going to get ice cream?"

Stanley looks down, wondering how long Chord has been standing there. "No, I'm too fat."

Another rising sun emerges. Chord sits up in his seat, and his half-closed eyes look out at red canyons complemented by the rising orange giant. Beauty. *It's as if with each morning comes a new world. From flat, dusty plains to rolling grassy hills to deep canyons. If only life within our invisible boundaries could present such a variety of beauty as life on the road. It's strange that the so-called American dream was created by the same people who traveled across the land when it was flourishing with natural beauty. Smog and pollution, radio towers, and electric cables were only a hope for the future. The grass is always greener.*

As Chord pans the view, he notices Stanley standing at the edge of the canyon, seemingly soaking in the vastness. Chord exits the rig and, with a crackling stretch of his body, starts toward Stanley. The closer he gets, the more he can see that Stanley is fidgeting and upset.

Stanley hears the dry crunch of Chord's footsteps approaching and, as though he has been waiting for Chord to arrive, exclaims out into the open world before him, "Our bad deeds and awful addictions are always haunting us and challenging our way of life!" He turns and looks at Chord. "Oh, Lord, help him see my will. I don't want to hurt anybody, Chord. I'm a good man." Stanley looks back out into the world. His silhouette stands in the blaring sunlight at the edge of the abyss. "I crave the fear of a child. Absolute power. End my suffering. Push me! I can't stop. Oh, Lord, work through this young man. Make him the instrument of my destruction!"

Chord stands for a moment in a state of numb wonder. He turns toward the rig, and sitting in the cab are the gunshot victim and the old woman. They stare at Chord with frozen calm.

After death, are we monsters or men?

—4—

The road has become villainous. Chord walks slowly with a dry, salty residue of what was once sweat caked along his forehead. His lips are cracked and dry. The sun stares down at him, judging him. It has been three days since he departed from Matthias.

The road disappears at the horizon with not a sign of deliverance. The gunshot victim and old woman follow. *Hell. Purgatory.* The blurry sight of heat baking the sandy red ground, baking Chord, is constant. *Am I alive? Is this my afterlife?* Chord's mind is suffering from his body's lack of food and water. *All this death around me. It's always in moments of extreme desperation that you just want to be a child again and feel the comfort of your parents' embrace.*

Chord stops walking. He turns and stares at the old woman and the gunshot victim. He sees beyond them the road he has just traversed. *Or is that the way I was going?* Chord turns again, and standing before him are the old woman and the gunshot victim. The road is baking in the distance, leading to the same empty place. They smile at Chord. Chord screams at them. His voice breaks. "Why are you doing this to me? Why?" Chord sobs empty, dry tears. "Please help me. Please." Chord falls to his knees and then onto his back. He stares up at the sky.

Stanley walks up and leans over Chord. "God didn't forgive me. He won't forgive. Just float away with the clouds." Stanley looks up at the sky.

"Stanley?"

"Am I?"

"Maybe. Maybe you're dead. I told you about the Lord and his mysteries." Chord screams incoherently, and his eyes close.

Chord's mother and father sit at their breakfast table. It's quiet. Broken eggshells lie abandoned next to the oven as their insides slowly fry in a pan. If only a mother hen knew what became of her children.

Chord's mother holds the wireless home phone in her hand as she slowly sips from her cup of coffee. She glances down at her cell phone, which rests silently next to her empty plate. Chord's father stares into his coffee mug as if searching for meaning. If only a cup of coffee could communicate the secret meaning of life. Chord's father speaks without looking up from his mug.

"He's not going to call."

"He might."

"His phone was turned off. He hasn't paid his bill for the month."

"They don't cancel service for missing one month of payments."

"He's going to lose his job! He went crazy!"

"Oh, stop it! You always put him down. He didn't want that stupid job anyway!"

"That's just perfect. So my life was stupid?"

"No, that's not what I'm saying. He just wanted something else."

"We all want something else! We all want millions of dollars. Some people just don't get what they want. We all want to live our dreams! There comes a point when life reminds you that dreams only exist when you're asleep."

"That's not true."

"No? How's your career going?"

"How unfair."

"Life is unfair! We worked and sacrificed everything so our son could run away and ruin his life!" Chord's father becomes red in the face and chokes on each breath. "I was so proud of him."

Chord's mother drops the phone and puts her head in her hands.

Chord's father walks over to her, and they embrace. "I love you so much."

"I love you. Why did he do this?"

"Don't worry. The detectives will find him." Chord's father stands up and turns over the cooking eggs. "You sit. I'll finish up here and serve you for a change." He winks and smiles.

"I guess I can get used to that." Chord's mother smiles a bit and looks down at her phone.

Chord's father looks at the frying eggs. They sizzle and pop. He looks through the eggs. He remembers.

Chord was just an infant. He began to cry in his crib. Chord's mother and father were asleep. Chord's young mother rolled over to Chord's father and gently shook him. "It's your turn. I was just up with him."

Chord's father groaned in anger and frustration. "I have to be up in two hours to play music for this producer, and then I have to go to the academy."

"I understand that, but I will be home all day with the baby, and I need to sleep too."

Chord's father tore the covers off of himself and stormed over to Chord's crib. He gently wrapped his son in a blanket and held him, rocking gently to the song in his mind. Chord was quiet, and his father slowly placed him in the crib.

The second Chord was down, he began to cry again. Chord's father whispered with rage, "Go to fucking sleep! I wish you were never born!" He looked up and clenched his fists. Then he breathed, gently picked Chord up, and rocked him gently to sleep.

"I think the eggs are done!" Chord's mother exclaims.

Chord's father comes back from his memory and reenters the present moment. "I'm sorry."

"Don't be sorry."

"I'm so sorry." Chord's father puts the eggs onto his wife's plate. "I have to go to the bathroom." He hurries out of the room.

Detective Tim Miller sits at his desk, eating Chinese food from a cardboard container with a plastic fork. He's a big man, at least six foot two and 250 pounds, wearing a dark brown suit with a white shirt and brown tie. He has a long face and a full black mustache, which has some grease and food clinging to it. His hair is cut short but is thick and salt-and-peppered. His desk is scattered with manila file folders marked with different names and numbers. The screen-saver icon on his computer bounces from top to bottom and side to side on the screen. It's a picture of a golf ball. The folder he is eating over has the name Samson written on the tab.

The phone on his desk rings. Miller stares at it and forks another heap of food into his mouth. The phone rings again, and then it's interrupted and stops. Miller looks back down at his food.

"Miller!" a voice calls from the other room of the office. "Miller, we've got something!"

In walks Detective James Hallorand. He's a shorter man with long hair bunched into a messy bun at the back of his head. His face has about five days' worth of stubble on it. He is in great physical condition and is wearing a fitted button-down shirt and tight slacks. His tie is loosely fastened around his collar.

"When are you going to cut your hair, Hal? You look like a damn hipster."

"I am a hipster. We got the kid's car. In Missouri."

"Anything suspicious?"

"Just the car. Missouri PD says it has damage consistent with what Stolsky said. So when are we going?"

"They aren't going to let us go for just a car. Nothing suspicious?"

"A phone! They found a phone in the grass by the car. Unknown who it belongs to. They are being really cooperative with the investigation and haven't touched anything yet."

"All right. I'll call the boss and see what we can do."

Chord opens his eyes. He's lying on the side of the road. The sun is high over him. He wonders how long he has been lying there. His lips are dry, and his skin has collected dust. He pushes himself to his feet and peers down the road in each direction, unsure which way he was heading. *Stanley was at the edge. Did I step from some metaphorical edge? Is this the plummet?*

Chord chooses a direction and begins to walk, a living zombie. *Do these things happen? As our lives progress, we experience such atrocities. Can this be real? This desolate road. It's endless. Some people say life is short, but it's like this road. You can't see over the horizon. Surrounded by vastness. All we can do is travel at our own pace, with no notion of whether we will ever see the horizon or when.*

As Chord walks, a man alone, an aimless wanderer surrounded by nothing and everything, he glances back, and the boy and the woman are following him with an all-knowing calm in their faces. He feels a deep sense of fear unlike any fear he has ever encountered in the physical world. The fear slowly transforms into an empty sadness of one lost and alone. Chord thinks of Samantha.

Samantha sits at a small table in her favorite coffee shop, typing on her laptop. A cup of iced coffee waits on the table, resting in a small puddle of condensation, neglected. She stops typing and glances around the shop, an observer. She smiles at a dog waiting outside tied to a bench. *Love. Unconditional.* The dog stares at its owner while he orders his beverage.

Samantha looks back down at the screen and reads her last entry.

This empty chair,
my companion,
talk to me.
Tell me what you see.
I too know the feeling,
my wooden companion.
Once alive, free.
Remember the wind,
the spring
who broke you down.
You're not alone.
Once full of life,
skinned alive,
molded to fit in.
Who is our carpenter?

Samantha feels a vibration in her pant leg. She reaches into her pocket and pulls out her cell phone. "Hello? Oh, hi, Ben. No, I'm not busy. Oh, did you? Well, I had a good time too. Yeah, I'd love to. What time? Okay." Samantha places her phone down on the table and smiles.

She hasn't heard from Chord since he left. She texted and called him to no avail. That was when she fell back into what was comfortable and what she knew. Ben was another online match.

Chord sits at the side of the road. The sun slowly kisses the horizon. He has a shirt wrapped around his head. He sits staring into his backpack in the dirt. The gun's cold, malevolent black steel seems impervious to the heat of the day. An insidious look befalls Chord's eyes. He thinks of

Stanley at the edge of the cliff, the edge of all his salvation, the edge of his end or his beginning. He imagines Manny standing on an unstable perch with a power cord tied around his neck. Then there is the gun. Three pounds of pressure. An inch of movement with his trigger finger.

Chord looks up at the boy and the old woman. He looks back down at the gun. "This is what you want?" He looks back up, and the boy and woman are gone.

He hears a car heading toward him in the distance, toward the setting sun. Chord quickly pulls the shirt off his head, throws it into the backpack, and hops to his feet. The sound of the approaching car seems to somewhat revitalize Chord.

A small red car screams toward Chord. He can hear the distorted music. He raises his arms and waves his hands in a sign of distress. The car skids to a stop, throwing pebbles and dust into the air, breaking any sense of calm in the open, empty land. A gentle putter from a leaky exhaust beckons Chord toward the car. Salvation?

Chord bends and peers into the passenger-side window of the small car. There is not an ounce of space available in the rear portion of the car. Clothes, garbage, sneakers, a guitar, an old-fashioned milkshake blender, a DVD player, and a small flat-screen television are slovenly jammed inside. Before Chord can speak, the driver, in an altruistic tone, exclaims, "Hey, man, hop in!" The driver is shirtless, is in his mid to early thirties, wears a pleasant smile, and has a fit upper body. His head is shaved, and his eyes are crystal blue and full of intensity.

Chord pulls open the door, and with a scraping, crunching pop, the door falls to the ground, yanking itself free from Chord's grasp. It seems forever, like a moment of silence at a funeral, that Chord and the driver stare at the severed door as it lies inert in the sand. The driver's eyes slowly pan from the slain door to focus on Chord's eyes. The pleasant smile is replaced with a stony expression.

"I'm so sorry." Chord is paralyzed with disbelief.

Just as he is about to make another attempt to show remorse, the driver bursts into uncontrollable laughter. Chord, torn from fright and disbelief, is now befuddled and still paralyzed.

"Oh man, that was what I needed! Oh man, you need to see your face!"

At that, the driver tears from the windshield his rearview mirror and turns it toward Chord. Chord jumps at the sudden demolition and then, seeing his pale and awestruck reflection, becomes infected with weak laughter. The driver drops the mirror into the passenger seat, still losing his breath to laughter, and exits the vehicle. Chord and the driver stand looking down at the door, and both ease down to a chuckle.

"As I said, I'm sorry about this."

"Eh, it's no bother. Let's just see if we can reattach it in some way. Otherwise, it will be an uncomfortable ride."

"Yeah, especially if it starts raining."

The two laugh again, and the driver extends his hand for a shake. "My name's Noah."

"Chord."

They lift the car door and align it in its rightful place.

"What are you doing out here?" Noah asks as he struggles to keep the door in place.

"Going for a walk."

"Pretty long walk, if you ask me. The world's too big to stay in one place, huh? Looks to me like you've been out here awhile. Hold the door up, and I'll run to the other side and see if there's some way to reattach it."

Noah climbs into the driver's side and starts fumbling around within the car to try to keep the door from falling off. "I've got it." Noah grabs the seat belt and loops it around the door handle and the seat's headrest. "Okay, let go; let's see if this holds."

Chord slowly lets the door go, and it is secure.

"Hop in!"

Chord reaches for the handle to pull the door open and then stops.

Noah laughs again and motions toward the window. "Literally hop in!"

Chord slips through the window and settles in the seat. "I hope the seat belt laws are lenient out here."

The car speeds off down the road. Chord glances back over his shoulder and watches the dead boy and the woman left standing in the dust shrink away until they are eaten by the horizon.

"You leave something behind?" Noah asks.

"I hope so."

"Sounds heavy."

"Yeah. You may have come just in time."

"So where are you heading?"

"I don't know, but I could use some water."

"Well, although it may not seem so, I myself do have a destination: Colorado City, Arizona." Noah reaches under his seat and pulls out a military canteen. He hands it to Chord. "You cool with that?"

"Sure. Sounds like an interesting place."

"No, it doesn't." Noah laughs. He can tell Chord has something bouncing around his mind.

A life of plans and agendas overcomplicates the simplicity and beauty in each day, Chord thinks. *Living only to ensure tomorrow's life is dying one day at a time. Detaching oneself from learned patterns and behavior is the only way to live. We must challenge ourselves. We must take ourselves to the edge of the abyss and stand before it with confidence and drive on. We must leap without fear.*

Ben is a well-built man in his midthirties. He has dirty-blond hair and brown eyes. He is a successful investment banker and an extremely kind man. When Samantha walks into the restaurant, his face lights up with a joyous smile. "I'm so glad you were able to make it."

Samantha gives him a kiss on the cheek. "Of course. I had fun last week."

"Yeah?" Ben laughs. "I wasn't sure how cheesy bowling on a first date would seem."

"Not at all."

"Shall we sit?" He puts his hand on the small of Samantha's back and leads her toward their table. He pulls her chair out for her to sit, and the waiter takes over the rest.

"Have you been here before?" Samantha asks.

"Yes. The food is delicious."

"Not to mention the ambiance to impress your date." Samantha smiles.

"Well, there is that too, of course." Ben reaches over the table to rest his hand in hope that Samantha will grab hold of it.

Samantha notices the move but, for some reason, doesn't take the bait. The waiter comes by, and they order their drinks. Ben orders a gin martini, and Samantha orders a chardonnay. "So anything interesting happen to you over the week?" he asks.

"Not really. Did some writing. My life is kind of dull. What about you? Any exciting news in banking?"

Ben laughs. "Not much. I guess my week was kind of dull too. Except there was a new feeling of excitement at the thought of seeing you again." He smiles.

Samantha slides her hand forward, and her fingers entwine with Ben's.

The sun rises slowly with majesty when you stop to look at it.

Noah and Chord are parked by the side of the road a mile from the state line in Arizona, still surrounded by desert and red rock canyons. Noah is asleep in the car, and Chord sits out on a boulder, watching the sunrise.

Noah walks from the vehicle to where Chord is. Chord looks like a thinking man as Noah approaches. Without looking away from the rising sun, Chord says, "It's a beautiful country."

"Yes, it is."

"Not many people notice it."

"Not many take the time."

"There's so much other nonsense to look at in the cities. We're losing the meaning of things in the real world."

"Well said." Noah walks back to the car and reaches into the trunk. He walks back over to Chord with an urn. "This is as good a spot and moment as any." He twists open the urn, reaches in, and pulls out a handful of ash and bone particles. "Semper fi, brother." Noah releases the handful of his friend.

Chord watches quietly with interest. The ash is carried up and dispersed by the wind in a final dance. The silence is loud, and the gentle, warm breeze seems to penetrate Chord's and Noah's souls, carrying a piece of each of them off with the remains of Noah's friend. *Sometimes we don't need to understand a moment to share it.*

"Well, let's go deliver the rest of David," Noah says.

Samantha opens her eyes. She's lying in bed next to Ben. She looks over at the bedside clock. It's five thirty in the morning. She rolls back over and whispers into his ear, "Ben, I'm going to go home."

"Okay. Call me later." Half asleep, Ben kisses her.

Samantha gets up and slips into her dress. She collects her various items and begins to exit the apartment, when Ben leaps up and grabs her.

"Don't think I'm going to let you off that easily!" He kisses her deeply, and she embraces him. They separate and look at each other. "Sorry for the morning breath."

"Jeez, I was going to be nice and not mention it, but ugh!" She's playful, but inside, she feels a regret she can't understand. She's moving too fast.

"Hey, that's not really nice. You know, I may be falling for you."

Samantha takes a step back, visually affected.

"I hope that's all right."

She smiles with a hint of fear. She thinks of Chord and feels somewhat ashamed but can't understand why. "It's more than all right. It's just—I'm sorry. I have to go. I have to feed my cat."

"Okay. I didn't mean to upset you. I know we've only known each other a couple of weeks."

"Please don't apologize. I just need to go. I'll call you."

"Okay."

Samantha exits the building and stops on the sidewalk. She takes a deep breath and begins to walk home. "What just happened?" She speaks aloud to herself. "He almost said it. *Love*. What if he had? Oh man. Love. What if he had? Why would that be bad? No, it's ridiculous. We've only known each other five days."

Samantha stops at the corner to wait for a crossing signal. "You did just sleep with him. Only five days. There is something different, though. Is there? There's something." She looks east, and from where she is stopped, there is an open view of the rising sun over the horizon between the buildings. Its light brings a warmth that caresses her face, and then a gentle, warm breeze touches her heart. She thinks about Chord in that moment and the feeling she has for him.

She looks down at her phone and at the last message she sent to Chord, as if maybe in that moment, he will finally respond. *Without some disappointments, we might not know what we are looking for.*

Samantha turns around and walks back to Ben's. *No one knows how things are going to end, so we must not be afraid to trust the moment.*

Chord's father walks back and forth, pushing his lawn mower across the overgrown front lawn. A blue car pulls up in front of the house, and two men in suits exit the vehicle—cops. Chord's father knows what they are the minute they exit the vehicle. He kills the mower's engine and hesitantly walks toward the two men, expecting the worst news of his life.

Detective Miller starts. "Mr. Samson?"

"Yes. Is my son all right?"

"Sir, I'm Detective Miller, and this is Detective Hallorand."

"I know who you guys are. Is my son alive?"

"Sir, we don't know," Miller says, and Chord's father's body seems to deflate. "We found his car, sir. It was on the side of the road in Missouri. There didn't seem to be signs of a struggle. We believe his phone was left in the grass near the car, but there didn't seem to be anything suspicious."

"So there are no leads as to where he might be?"

"All we have is that he is most likely heading west."

Chord's mother glances out the window when she realizes the mower has stopped. After seeing her husband talking with the two suits, she runs out to them.

"What's happening? Where's Chord? Is he okay?" She weeps the last words.

Chord's father grabs her as she collapses to her knees. "They don't know anything. They just found his car in Missouri. He's fine." As Chord's father says those words, he feels a sudden rush of anger. "He's just a spoiled brat who is causing all this trouble because he can't grow up!"

"Shut up! That's what drove him away!"

"Sir, ma'am, please," Miller says.

"Mind your own business," Chord's father says. "You think I'm the reason he can't hack it?"

"You pushed him too hard! He didn't want this life.

Your life." Chord's mother breaks into full sobs, and his father holds her close to him and strokes her head.

"He'll be fine. We'll get through this. I'm sorry, guys. Thanks for the update. Why don't you take our number? That way, you don't have to waste your time driving out here."

"Yes, sir. If there is anything you need, I'll leave my card. Don't hesitate."

Chord's father and the detectives exchange their information, and then they part. Detective Miller turns back around. "Sir, do you know anyone your son might be going to see in Missouri or some other state? Any friends or family?"

Chord's mother and father turn around to address the detectives, and his father says, "We don't have any family out of state. I don't know if he has any friends."

"Okay. Thanks, sir. Ma'am. Just thought it might be a lead. Good day."

The detectives get back in their car, and Chord's parents walk back into the house. The mower sits inert on the half-cut lawn.

Chord and Noah are a few miles from their destination, driving through a suburb of Arizona, when Chord asks, "So you were a marine?"

"I am a marine." Noah smiles.

"Yes, of course. I'm sorry. Is this part of your job?"

"No, I'm not active anymore." Noah's infectious, large smile retreats into a calm expression. "I lost a few men and thought I'd bring them back home. It was a deal we made with each other."

"I'm sorry to hear that. So you live in the Midwest?"

"No, I live back east. New York."

"No shit. Me too."

"I know."

"What? Do I have the accent?"

"No, I saw your picture on the news."

Chord feels his heart throb into his throat.

Noah looks at him and smiles, and Chord can't speak. "Yes, you are on the news. AWOL cop. Your boys are looking for you."

"You must be mistaken. I'm just—"

"Going for a walk. I got that." Noah returns to his wide grin.

"Well."

"Well?"

"Look, I don't want any issues. I'm just doing my thing, and I'll get out at the next stop." Chord shifts nervously.

"Don't be ridiculous. We all have an adventure. I'm honored to share part of yours. Just promise me it's not an ending-your-life adventure." Noah looks at Chord as though he has been able to read his mind the whole drive.

Chord's heart begins to throb again. "What?" *It's so much easier to lie to yourself than to others.* "What would you think that do I'd that to me?"

"Ha-ha, first time using your new mouth?" Noah laughs as though they are discussing getting a tattoo. "It's just what you said when you were looking back at the horizon after I picked you up: 'You may have come just in time.'" Noah looks back at Chord.

"What were you—CIA? Jesus."

"Not Jesus—Noah. And tell me I'm wrong. That bag

you haven't let go of has a little extra weight on the right side. Your nine-millimeter, I presume."

"Okay. When you found me, that was where my mind was at. I was dehydrated!"

Noah bursts into laughter. "Oh man, you are a riot! Look, life isn't that bad. Think about it. I've got David, Jimmy, and Jose in my trunk. They would trade places with you in a second." For the first time, Noah becomes solemn. "Do your parents know where you are?"

Chord looks at him. He feels a connection with Noah, as if he is part of Noah, or Noah is part of him, and he feels that if something happened to him, Noah would ache.

"You should call them. I've already delivered the remains of two of my brothers. It was as if their parents never found peace, or couldn't, until they knew their children's definite whereabouts."

"I will."

"Good. I think we are here." Noah pulls the car to the side of the road in front of a small house. In the driveway rests an old-model sedan with rust and worn tires.

"Oh. I guess I'll just wait here."

"No, no, no, you're coming in. Never let a man go into battle alone."

"I can't do this, man. This is too heavy. I'm already—"
"You're going to do it."

With that, Chord and Noah retrieve the urn from the trunk and ring the doorbell.

The dull-sounding doorbell brings with it a beautiful, bright-eyed young woman. She has dirty-blonde hair, blue eyes, a full figure, and clear, soft skin. Following behind her is a small boy with dusty-brown hair, big brown eyes, and a wide smile.

"May I help you?" she asks.

Noah smiles and looks at the young boy. "That must be Ace."

"How do you know that? Do I know you?"

"David used to talk about his son. He said he hoped you named him Ace. Did you?"

The woman's eyes well up with tears. "His name is Ace. Who are you?" She looks down at the urn, and it becomes harder for her to hold back emotion.

"I was with your husband, Sandy. I was with him when he died."

She begins to sob. Little Ace calls to her, and she lifts him up.

"I'm sorry to bring back these feelings, but we made a promise to each other."

Sandy wipes her eyes, which don't stop leaking, and composes herself as much as possible. "You must be Noah."

"How did you know?"

"He said his sergeant was my type. And he said if anyone survived that shithole, it would be you." Sandy forces a giggle. "His mother is here too. I took her in after we heard. Come in, please." She leads the way into the living room. It is a small house crowded with toys. "Which one are you?" Sandy asks, referring to Chord.

"I'm no one, ma'am."

"That's not true. He is a dear friend of mine. He keeps me strong." Noah smiles at Chord.

"Mama! One of David's friends is here!" Sandy calls out.

From the back room, a woman in her sixties walks in. "Oh. What do they want?"

"Hi, ma'am. I'm Noah. I was your son's sergeant. I was there when we came under attack."

"Why did you survive?"

"Mama!" Sandy says. "I'm sorry, Noah."

"It's okay. You're right. I guess I was spared to carry your son and the other sons back home."

"What do you mean 'back home'?" the older woman asks. "My son is dead."

"Yes, ma'am. These are his remains. We all agreed that whichever of us made it would hand deliver the remains to the family. I'm sorry."

"Tough job. Surviving."

"Mama!" Sandy says.

David's mother is fighting her tears with anger. Sandy is in shock. Noah accepts the abuse and maybe even believes he deserves it.

Chord is like a statue. There are so many levels of intensity in life and so many ways to react. *How should one react? That is the fingerprint of our soul.* He thinks of Manny. He thinks of Samantha. He thinks of what brought him to this place. Then, out of the corner of his eye, he sees them looking in from the back room—the gunshot victim and the old woman, smiling.

"Yes, ma'am. It is. Your son was a great man. He died with honor and without fear."

Sandy starts sobbing.

"He died thinking of his family and hoping you would be well."

Tears fall from David's mother's eyes.

"He died saving my life. This is all I can do for him. Thank you for my life."

With that, David's mother sobs and hugs Noah. "Thank you for bringing my boy home."

Chord and Noah sit quietly as they drive away from David's home. *How do you weigh such a thing? The loss. The honor. There are people in this world who will give up their lives in one way or another without asking for anything in return. These are the people who should be modeled.* Chord feels ashamed that Noah figured him out in a matter of minutes. Ashamed that he left behind people and a life that was given to him. *There are men and boys dying in faraway lands in support of the life I am running from*, Chord thinks.

The car jolts to the right and slides to a stop. Noah quickly leaves the car and, with the door still open, walks off into the desert. Chord is shocked out of his thoughts and consumed by the dust stirred up. He feels like the inside of a magic trick, and Noah is making him disappear. Chord really wonders if Noah can read minds.

He reaches for the handle and pushes the car door open. It falls to the ground, dangling by the seat belt, which is wrapped around the headrest. Chord steps over the door and exits the vehicle. He sees Noah silhouetted by the bright desert about one hundred feet from the car, sitting in the sand. Standing beside him are the gunshot victim and the old woman. Chord approaches slowly. The old woman gestures with her head for Chord to go to Noah. Then the ghosts both stand with their chins to their chests as Chord sits next to Noah, as if they are attending a wake for the living.

"Hey, man, are you okay?"

Noah rubs his face with the palms of his hands and takes a deep breath. "Yeah. It gets easier and easier. I hate myself for that." Noah looks at Chord and then off into the vast land.

"I don't really know what to say to you." Chord looks down at his knees. It drives him crazy when he knows something should be said but can't figure it out. It's like a riddle that everyone figures out but him, and the others just sit and laugh. "Meeting you might have saved me. I know I'm just a whiny cop. Full of shit. Scared to death. I don't compare to the men you lost. But you saved me."

Noah's eyes seem to come back from wherever they were, and he turns and looks at Chord.

No words are necessary. Noah gets up and pulls Chord up. "I have a cooler in the trunk. Let's have a beer."

They walk over to the car, and Noah opens the trunk. A small cooler rests inside. He opens the cooler. There are four cans of beer and no ice. Noah looks back at Chord and smiles. "They might be a little warm."

Chord slowly applies the brake and pulls into a gas station. Noah is asleep in the passenger seat. Chord's mind swims with thoughts. The gunshot victim and the old woman are waiting in front of a pay phone next to the gas station's restroom. They've been around ever since David's house. The gunshot boy puts his thumb to his ear and his pinkie to his mouth, signifying a phone.

"Yeah, I see you. I'm not haunted; I'm aggravated." Chord parks the car and quietly opens the door, watching to make sure he doesn't wake Noah. Noah doesn't flinch.

When Chord turns back toward the phone, the boy and woman are gone.

Chord's mother is lying in bed when the phone rings. "Hello?"

"Mom?"

"Chord, is that you? Oh my God, Chord, where are you? Are you okay? What's going on?"

"Mom, take a breath. I'm sorry. I'm fine."

"Take a breath? We thought you were dead! The last time I spoke to you ... Why are you doing this?"

"Mom, I'm sorry. I just needed to get away." Chord can hear his father in the background.

"Is that him? He's okay?"

"Pick up the other phone! He's okay!" his mother says.

"Chord, you're okay?" his father asks once on the line.

"I'm okay, Dad. I'm sorry."

"Don't be sorry. Just thank God you're okay. Where are you?"

"In Arizona somewhere."

"Arizona!" his mother and father exclaim at the same time.

"You might still be able to keep your job, but you have to come home now," his father says. "Do you need money? We can send you some."

"Dad, please just give—"

"Don't scare him off the phone! Just shut up about that damn job," his mother says.

"Well, it's import—"

"Dad! Stop for a minute, please. I know you are worried about me. Just give it a rest for a minute. I'm going to be okay. I miss you guys."

"We miss you, honey. We are sorry if we did something," his mother says.

"You guys didn't do anything. I need a little more time. Mom, I need you to find something for me. It's a phone number. I'll explain everything to you when I see you. I love you both, and I want to thank you for all you've done for me. I'm sorry I'm asking for more, but I must."

The city is alive. The day is warm but not hot. The sidewalks are littered with brunch-goers sipping coffee and chatting. There is cheering from inside the small restaurants as patrons watch a soccer game. Samantha and Ben sit at a small table, holding hands and conversing over the cheers of the crowd.

After he met Samantha, Ben knew she was the woman for him. She is like a beautiful landscape that reveals itself slowly from beyond a curvy mountain road. All the romantic movies were right. It was love at first sight. Every time he says something clever, Samantha smiles and presses his hand slightly in hers. He never wants to cease amusing her. He loves her smile, which is full and from the heart.

She feels a strong bond with Ben too. She imagines him coming home from work, and she has prepared a meal for him. They sit together at their table with a fine bottle of red wine, breathing in the romantic air. Samantha never has thought ahead more than a day or two. What is this that she feels? Is it friendship she seeks?

They sit alone among the crowd. Sifted through love, they are two gold pieces glimmering among pebbles. This is happiness.

"I'm glad I didn't scare you off the other morning."

"I'm glad too." Samantha smiles.

"I didn't mean to startle you. You just have this way of melting away my insecurities. You make me feel strong in ways I've never understood."

Samantha smiles. She thinks of Chord for some reason. She doesn't know how to respond. "Well, you make me feel beautiful." She laughs out loud. "And embarrassed."

Ben smiles, never losing eye contact with her. The waiter takes their orders, and they sit hand in hand, enjoying each other's company without words.

They eat and smile and glow together. *Where does this feeling originate?* Samantha thinks. *It's like the first journey of a sea turtle after it's born. Straight to the ocean. Is love the instinct we humans share that isn't learned?* She thinks of Chord's calloused hands and how her fingers felt twisted in his. It makes her uncomfortable to sit holding Ben's soft hand. She's worried she will hurt him.

Noah's car seems to float down the interstate atop the troubles that once threatened to end Chord's life. *That is the way of life. We can't find happiness; we can only live it.*

"Did you call your parents?"

"Yeah. And my job."

"How did that go?" Noah laughingly asks.

"Well, I may lose my job. I really don't know."

"You want me to drive you to a train or something?"

"No. I was hoping to help you finish your mission and get these guys home."

Noah turns and smiles at Chord.

Noah is good at that—not needing to say anything but expressing himself perfectly. *That's part of the problem in this world*, Chord thinks. *People talk so much but rarely ever have anything to say.* Chord continues. "I'm afraid to go back. I feel different out here. My shrink said that if I have these extreme ups and downs, I should consider medication." He smiles at Noah. "But that feels like it was another world. Another time."

—5—

The door is dented and dirty. The doorjamb is cracked and barely holding the door shut. Noah knocks. Behind the door, they can hear a daytime talk show blaring and kids screaming and banging. Noah knocks again. The peephole goes dark.

"Who is it?"

"Hi, ma'am. My name is Noah."

"What do you want? I don't know any Noah!"

"Are you Becky Roberts?"

"She isn't here. You cops?"

"No, ma'am, I'm a friend of her husband, Jimmy Roberts."

"What do you know about Jimmy? You dropping off money for that no-good nigga? Matter of fact, why don't you tell him to get his skinny black ass back here and handle his shit?"

"Jimmy's dead. Died in Afghanistan. I'm here to deliver his remains to his wife, Becky."

Amid the noise from the TV and kids, there is silence from the woman behind the door. "Will you kids be quiet and turn that damn TV down?"

They hear the sound of one lock being unlocked, followed by another and another. The door opens slowly. A young black woman with tired, watery eyes looks over the two men in front of her. What a sight they must be.

"Jimmy said he was going to get a job to pay for the baby. Then his chicken-shit ass heard it was twins, and I never heard from him again. I've been doing this alone. Things I can't even talk about because I don't want them to be real, and you come here telling me he died in Afghanistan? Like what? Like a soldier? Fighting in some land away from his pregnant wife? Never writes. Never sends a check. I sell my body to buy formula. Let these dirty niggas rub up on me. Should I be proud of him?"

Noah stares at her. His eyes absorb her hate and pain and whittle it down. "He wrote a letter to you every month. He couldn't understand why you never responded. He sent money. How do you think I knew this address? I have a letter here with this address. He never had a chance to send it."

"Who the fuck is that at the door?" a deep voice shouts from the back room.

Becky jumps as if she forgot she wasn't alone. Her face is distorted with disbelief. She tries to answer but doesn't know what words to use. She is still unsure who exactly is at the door.

Sometimes, when there are no answers, it's easy to hate and to place blame. Resent grows on us like a fungus until we are no longer recognizable, Chord thinks.

"Bitch! Who's at the door?" A large white man with a dirty beard and pockmarks stomps into view and toward Becky. He's more than six feet tall and weighs more than two hundred pounds. "Oh shit, girl. You got customers? Next time, tell me that shit." The big man slaps the back of Becky's head. It seems a common interaction, except on this occasion, the slap knocks loose the tears Becky is trying to keep hidden from Chord and Noah. "Oh, don't cry, silly bitch."

"Is this your pimp, Becky?" Noah asks.

As Noah speaks, something down the hallway catches Chord's attention. Manny is standing against the wall, watching Chord.

"Maybe he knows something about the money Jimmy sent," Noah says.

"Who the fuck is this skinny bitch? You must be crazy," the man says.

"Where's the money Jimmy sent?" Noah asks.

"You better get your ass out of my hallway."

"J, it's okay, baby. I'll get rid of these guys," Becky says.

"You ain't customers," J says. Then he turns toward Becky. "And men are talking bitch!" With that, J backhands Becky in her mouth. She falls backward and lands on her back. The kids begin to cry.

Chord, who is fixated on Manny, is yanked back into the reality of the moment. Before Becky hits the ground, Noah's fist collides with J's throat, and his other fist lands with bloody impact on J's nose. Noah keeps moving forward as J stumbles back. Noah unleashes fury. J has no chance to defend himself. His legs collapse from under him, and Noah falls forward on top of the big man.

Chord realizes he is still at the door, frozen. Becky sits up, reaches out, grabs Chord's leg, pulls him into the apartment, and shuts the door. As the situation unfolds, Chord's mind flashes back to a memory of his father.

Chord was just about seventeen years old and graduating from high school, when he saw a side of his father he never had imagined existed. He was speaking with his father about college and his plans for the future. He told his father he would go to community college to get his associate's degree but then wanted to major in writing.

"But I thought you were going to take the test and become an officer." Chord's father looked at Chord with disdain.

"Well, that was an option, Dad, but I wasn't certain about it."

"So instead, you want to wait tables until you're forty. No medical coverage. No future!"

"Well, I don't know. I will have to work while I go to school anyway."

"You have to grow up. These silly dreams are a waste of time. There are a million people striving to be famous writers. You aren't any better than those people. It's a sad life, and you'll end up with nothing."

"But you always said you loved making music."

"And then I grew up! Because it was a pipe dream! I got a realistic career and a family!"

"Well, I don't want to be a fucking cop and afraid to go after my dreams! A loser!"

Chord's father smacked Chord in the face, causing Chord to fall back off his feet. His lips bled. He was stunned. He mentally composed himself as best as he could and looked up at his father with anger and defeat.

"I'm sorry, Chord. I didn't mean to … I mean, I just

don't want you to follow some childish dream. It only ends with regrets." Chord's father reached down to help Chord get up.

"I'm fine." Chord got up on his own and walked away.

Noah lets out a guttural scream, and Chord snaps back into the moment. Chord pulls Noah off J. His face is smothered in blood, and his eyes are already swelling. "You okay, man?" Chord asks.

Noah looks at Chord. His eyes tell a violent, sad story. "I'm sorry, Chord." Noah takes a deep breath. "Becky, are you okay?"

"Yes." Becky is awestruck. She looks at J on the floor. "Jason?" She isn't sure how to feel.

"Go make sure your kids are okay," Noah says.

Becky looks down at Jason, who is taking deep, gasping breaths and beginning to moan.

"Becky, your kids. Chord, I need your help. Go find a towel. I'll be right back."

Chord stands over Jason with a brown towel in his hands, watching Becky comfort her kids on the couch. Standing beside them are Manny, the dead boy, and the dead woman. There is sadness in their eyes.

Noah enters the apartment with rope and a plastic hose. He rolls Jason over and binds his hands behind his back and then binds his feet. "Help me drag him to the kitchen."

Chord grabs Jason's feet, and Noah pushes.

"Becky go into the bedroom with the kids," Noah says.

Jason is starting to regain consciousness. Noah aligns him so his head is parallel with the sink. Then he attaches the hose to the faucet and turns it on. Noah then ties another piece of rope firmly around Jason's forehead and down the center of his back to his hands.

"What do you want from me?" Jason asks.

"Oh, not feeling very confident now? I want to know what you did with the money Jimmy sent."

"I don't know anything about that, mothafucker."

"Give me the towel," Noah says, and Chord hands Noah the towel. Noah soaks the towel in the sink with the makeshift hose and then flops it over Jason's face. "Chord, go get the cushions from the couch."

Chord pulls the cushions from the couch and runs back over to Noah, still in awe of the moment.

"Okay, leave the cushions here, and lift his legs as high as you can." Noah stuffs the cushions under Jason's body so his lungs are at a higher point than his mouth and nose. He then points the stream of water down over Jason's covered face. Jason pumps his body and tries to wiggle away. "Hold his legs!"

Chord holds on to his legs. Jason chokes, spits, and gasps.

Noah kinks the hose and removes the towel. "You see what's going on here? You're the motherfucker! Now, this can go on until you start breathing water or until you tell me the truth."

"I stole her mail. Aight! Shit, but there ain't no fucking money. That shit's gone."

"Do you have proof?"

"What fuckin' proof?"

Noah throws the towel down. It clings to Jason's face, and the water flows. "I can do this all night. You better grow gills, you fat fuck." Noah points the hose back into the sink, and Jason coughs blood, water, and spit and gasps for air.

"I kept his letters!"

Sometimes it's not the method that is horrific but the truth it reveals, Chord thinks.

"Enough!" Becky stands behind Chord with a small handgun outstretched. "That's enough. Get away from him."

"That's a good girl, baby. Shoot these mothafuckers."

"Becky, be careful with that," Noah says.

"Just shut up, and slowly walk outta my damn life!"

Chord and Noah slowly walk toward the door with their hands held in the air. Becky follows them, being sure not to get too close.

"What are you gonna do now?" Chord's confusion turns to empathy.

"You take that urn. I'm gonna burn those letters. J isn't bad. He just in bad. We all are. He's all I got."

"What about your kids?" Noah asks.

"You don't even know. This is life. This is what we know. You all don't know what it is over here. You're just passing through. I don't want to mourn Jimmy. It's too damn hard. He's a no-good nigga who left his pregnant wife."

The door closes. Noah stares at the door. Without an ounce of emotion, he says, "On to the next."

Compartmentalization.

Every ten miles traveled, Chord sees the dead boy and woman standing at the side of the road. Manny has joined them. Noah is quiet, different, more focused on the road and driving. His brow is flat and stiff. His jaw is locked. Looking at him is like looking at a wax statue.

The burdens we carry carry us. Chord thinks about all the men and women who fight and die for their country. All the families and friends lost. *Why are we always fighting?* he thinks. *There they are again.* The ghoulish stalkers are back. *It's like counting sheep.*

Chord looks over at Noah, who is still focused on the never-ending straight road to the horizon as if he's all alone in the car. Chord's eyes slowly close.

Detectives Miller and Hallorand stand at Chord's abandoned car, wearing white gloves. They have finished their investigation of the car, and the crime scene unit from Missouri are packaging Chord's leftover belongings for the detectives to take back to the city.

"So where do you guys go to have some fun around here?" Hallorand asks.

A crime scene officer looks up at Hallorand. "There's a nice place in—"

Hallorand's phone rings, and he answers it, interrupting the officer. "What's up, boss? He what? Jesus Christ. So what now? Do we bring this shit with us?"

Miller curiously looks at Hallorand. "What is it?"

Hallorand ignores Miller and continues the phone conversation. "Okay. So we'll bring all this back and have them impound the car here. Ten-four." Hallorand puts his phone in his pocket and addresses Miller. "Fucking kid called the precinct. He's in Arizona, and he's fine. There's no issue."

"Little prick. I mean, what the fuck?"

"So we pack up and go home. Case closed. Kid's probably gonna get canned."

Miller runs his hands through his hair. "What the hell is he doing in Arizona?" He seems disappointed. "Case closed. Just like that." They've been rendered useless.

The neon lights emit a ghostly hue. The dust from the dirt parking lot glows in the air. The music is loud and distorted. Sawdust is clumped in muddy piles on the floor. A stench of liquor and beer mixed with body odor and grease fills the air. Noah sits on a stool beside Jimmy's urn. Several empty pint glasses and shot glasses quietly watch Noah mumble to Jimmy's remains. Noah's head seems too heavy for his neck to support.

The crowd is transient, made up of truckers and travelers running or hiding out and some locals. It is an angry place filled with dark secrets and lost souls.

Noah looks down at his empty glasses. "Bartender, another round for my friend and me." He looks down at Jimmy's urn with an odd smile and sadness in his eyes.

"I think you've had enough, friend!" a voice from behind Noah exclaims.

Noah turns around slowly. Standing behind him is an enormous man. His face is rough and scarred. He is wearing a leather vest with a motorcycle club insignia.

"They're for my friend, big man." Noah taps the top of Jimmy's urn. "Isn't that right, Jimmy? You *urned* it." Noah bursts out into laughter, startling the big man. "Get it? Ha! Urned it!" Noah stops laughing slowly as his face twists into anguish, and he stares into the big man's eyes. Then he slowly turns back toward the bar. "Another round, please."

The big man is amped up from the startling outburst of laughter. When Noah turns his back on him, it infuriates the big man. He grabs Noah with a hand so massive that it easily wraps almost completely around Noah's neck and pulls Noah down from the stool onto the ground. The urn falls back too, scattering Jimmy's remains in a cloudy pile. Noah, facedown on his hands and knees, stares at the remains on the ground next to him.

The bartender cries out, "Will, that's enough!"

Noah begins to shovel the remains back into the urn with his hands. "Jimmy, I'm sorry. I'm sorry. Come on, man." He talks to the dusty pile of his friend. "Here we go. We're home. We made it home."

Will stands over Noah, seemingly disturbed by causing the remains to spill. He reaches gently down and pats Noah on the back. "Hey, man, I didn't mean for—"

Before he can finish, Noah swings up his head, smashing it into Will's face while simultaneously grabbing and pulling Will's ankles toward him. Will falls back hard, grasping at his face. Noah closes the top of the urn, places it gently on the bar, and turns toward Will.

Samantha sits alone at her favorite café. Her notebook sits in front of her. She lifts her pen, puts the tip to paper, and then stops. She looks up through the window at all the people walking by. Her pen meets paper again.

> All you busy people
> caught up.
> Do you have time for love?
> Is it a distraction?

I am free to love and consumed by it.
Is that fair?
Because I still think and wonder about the
fish lost to the sea.
How selfish can I be?

Samantha closes her notebook and looks off into the emptiness of the café. All the patrons are focused on their electronics, silent. *False connections.* She thinks of Ben. They are two fish swimming around this immense sea. She thinks of Chord. *Why can't I get you out of my mind?* She feels a sense of sadness.

Out on the sidewalk, looking in at Samantha, the seemingly homeless young woman stands staring at her with a smirk on her face, as though she's smiling at Samantha's sadness. Samantha sits up straight with nervousness. She takes quick breaths as her heart beats faster. She stares at the woman on the sidewalk, as if wanting to make some attempt to communicate. Then the woman walks away. Samantha sinks within herself and lets out a sigh.

She takes a deep breath and decides to confront the woman. Samantha quickly packs up her notebook and rushes out of the café in the direction of the woman. She scans the crowd of people traveling like lemmings to their destinations, unaware of the world around them, drowning in their singular sense of importance.

Samantha easily spots the woman walking away. The woman's steps are slow and frothy compared to the spry, necessary steps of the surrounding crowd. Samantha closes the distance between her and the woman. Still uncertain why or what she will say to her, Samantha calls out, "Melissa!"

The woman stops and turns. Samantha stands about five feet from her, and the two look at each other for a moment.

"You have some nerve following me." Melissa appears surprised, angry, and sad.   "Melissa, I—"

Melissa interrupts. "Don't talk to me like you know me. You don't have the right to speak to me. Looks like life has been kind to you, with your nice boots and pretty shirt. Fuck you!"

"Melissa, please. I'm sorry. Let me help you."

"What makes you think I need your help?" Melissa is yelling now and creating a scene. "What makes you think I need help at all? Because my face is dirty? Because I sleep in a shelter? Because you took everything from me, and now you feel guilty? You need help. That's why you followed me. You need to try to save me in order to save yourself. I'm not stupid, Sam. I lost everything. You only lost them. So sit in your café, and imagine a better life."

Samantha doesn't speak. Her mind is racing, and there is so much to say that it all blends and sticks together and becomes intangible. "Can I give you at least some money?"

"Keep it. I'm doing all right for myself. Besides, I'll probably use it for the wrong things."

Samantha drops her chin to her chest and looks down at the floor.

"Don't look so pathetic." Melissa stares at Samantha for a moment. Her eyes are no longer angry. It's as if they tell a sad yet happy story. "Fuck it. How much do you have on you?"

Samantha looks up, reaches into her bag, pulls out her

wallet, and empties the wallet of cash. "About a hundred and twenty."

Melissa reaches over and grabs the money, and Samantha grabs her hand and holds it. "Anytime you need, I'll be at this café on Thursdays and Fridays."

Melissa doesn't pull her hand away. It's as though Samantha's touch is something she didn't realize she longed for. "Thank you."

"Anytime. I'll be here. Even if it's just to talk." Samantha looks Melissa in the eye. "Or to yell at me."

Melissa smiles for the first time since their bizarre interaction. "I'll see you around." She turns and walks off.

The sound of shouting wakes Chord. He's lost in a sleepy daze, and it takes him a minute to realize he is in the parking lot of some random bar—a random bar people are scurrying out of. "Well, it's not on fire." There are a few men chuckling by the window at whatever is going on inside.

Chord starts to put the pieces together and swiftly exits the car, accidentally pushing off the car door dangling by the seat belt. He runs to the window and peers in. Noah is fending off a big man with a knife. Chord runs in.

"Hold on! Hold on!" Chord shouts at the big man. Noah is bloody and swollen. "Put the knife down! Put the fucking knife down, or I will shoot you!" Chord raises his gun, pointing it at Will.

"This crazy asshole attacked me!" the man yells.

"That's fine; just put down the knife! And, Noah, back off!"

"No can do, Chord. The enemy has a face."

"Noah, we will handle this; just back off." Chord slowly

moves toward Noah. "Look at me, Noah." Noah looks at Chord. "It's over, man." Chord looks at Will. "It's over." He puts his gun back in his waistband, raises his hands, and slowly walks in between Noah and Will. "It's over. We have to get Jose home." Chord pulls the stick from Noah's hand.

Will stares, perplexed, slowly lowering the knife.

Chord sees the urn standing on the bar next to empty glasses that haven't been broken. "The man in the urn died fighting alongside my friend Noah here." Chord speaks loudly, as if to address everyone still in the bar. "They are marines. Noah has one more friend to take back home. Then he's free of this burden. I'm sorry for your face, Will. I'm sure Noah is too." Chord continues to stare at Noah and Noah at Chord.

A police officer barges through the door and addresses the bartender. "What the heck is going on here, Al? I got calls of knife fights and all kinds of crazy stuff!" He turns and sees Chord, Noah, and Will. "Will, what have you gotten into now?"

"Nothing, Lou. I just tripped."

"Well, did you fall on that other fella?"

"I tried to catch him." Noah doesn't miss a beat.

Chord smiles, and Will bursts into laughter. Then Chord starts laughing, as does Noah.

"I oughta take y'all in for causing a disturbance!" Lou says.

"Thanks, Lou. I'm really sorry you were bothered." The bartender walks him to the door.

Will walks over to Chord. "Thank you."

"No problem."

Will looks at Noah. "Semper fi." Will pulls up his shirt

sleeve. Tattooed on his shoulder is *USMC*. "You get our brother home."

Chord feels a deep envy for the bond these men have. *But*, he thinks, *sometimes envy is ignorance. These men are bound by devastation. Like the Coliseum left standing in Rome. How do they come from hell and then live among the arbitrary wants of a society that doesn't appreciate their sacrifice? When will they find peace? How?*

Where do we go from here? I mean, the destination is set, but what good is that? The car putters down the long stretch of road, heading east, as if reluctantly going back the way it came. Chord is driving, and Noah sits with his eyes closed, his face bruised. Chord ponders his travels so far. *Running away to that which we ran from. I feel a sense of relief to be going back. Blend that with a sense of fear, confusion, and disgust.* Chord's inner dialogue leaves him still and staring off into the horizon.

Noah opens his eyes and looks over at Chord. "Aside from this hangover, I think we are going to have a gas issue."

Chord looks over to Noah and then to the gas gauge: empty. He looks to the empty land behind them, to the south, to the north, and in front of them. "Well, I think that means we have a long walk ahead of us." Up on the side of the road, Chord sees the old woman, the boy, and Manny waiting at what appears to be a dirt path. "Hold on; I'm going to take a right!"

"What! Where?"

"Right here!" Chord turns, and the car skids off the road onto the dirt. Chord sees a small trailer in the distance. "There!"

"How the hell did you see that? Good eye."

"The better question is, how the hell did we run out of gas?"

The old woman, the boy, and Manny are standing by an old trailer, smiling. The trailer is surrounded by all types of cacti: barrel, crimson hedgehog, chain fruit cholla, and brittlebush. To the left of the trailer, in the shade of a barrel cactus, stands a headstone. Chord sees an old woman sitting on a wooden bench made from an old car door resting on rocks.

"Maybe she'll have some gas, but I doubt it," Noah says.

Chord turns quickly toward him. "You see her?"

"What? Right there?"

"She's not dead?"

"That's not ruled out yet. Are you okay?" Noah looks perplexed.

"Yeah. Just this heat is getting to me." The car pulls up to the makeshift bench and woman and stops.

"You boys got robbed."

"Ma'am?" Noah says, and she lifts her hand slowly and points to the rear of the car. Noah sticks his head out the window and looks back. A long plastic tube is hanging from the gas hole. "Damn, someone siphoned our gas!"

"You boys got robbed." The woman has leathery brown skin with deep wrinkles. She smiles. Her eyes glisten with elation. "You boys need my help."

Noah speaks over Chord from the passenger side. "Do you have gas?"

"Come in, boys. Come."

Noah looks at Chord. Chord steps out of the car. Noah climbs over the driver's seat and out of the car.

"Beautiful plants," Chord says. "Didn't know they could grow so well in this land."

The old woman smiles at Chord. "This land. Surviving. Growth is amazing in all parts of this world. Come in." The woman smiles and walks into her trailer, leaving the door open.

A small cot and wood-burning stove are all that fill the trailer. The woman lays out some animal skin on the floor as seating for Chord and Noah. "My name is Kachina. I do not have much to offer. But everything. Sit, please." Chord and Noah sit on the floor, and she sits in a small wooden chair. "I have been waiting for you." Kachina looks to Chord. "You see our future. Our connection to one another." She moves over to a small table in the corner of the trailer and grabs a small plastic container. Then she walks over to Noah, opens the container, dips her finger into a greasy clear paste, and rubs it into Noah's facial wounds.

"Ma'am, I don't know what you mean," Chord says.

"You see them." She hands Noah the cream and sits back down. "You were led to me by the spirits. I've been waiting for you."

Noah looks at Chord.

Chord shakes his head in doubt, fear, and disbelief. "I don't know what led me here. Can you tell me?"

"Why are you here and not home finding love and settling down?"

Chord stares at Kachina without responding aloud and thinks, *That is the question. What am I doing out here? What are any of us doing anywhere? Life is a journey we all make. A trip down individual paths leading to uncertain destinations. But how uncertain? I'm a cop. I can meet a woman and settle.*

Or settle down. Have a family, battle debt, buy a house and car, and die happily ever after. Job, family, death. American dream. American reality show. American tragedy.

"You are strong and capable. I'm sure there are women looking for a young man like you." Kachina responds to Chord as though she's heard his thoughts.

"I don't know."

"You just don't realize it."

"Maybe, or maybe I don't want to settle down."

"What do you want then?"

Chord remembers his mother asking that same question. He remembers Samantha smiling in the morning and her dumb cat. "I'm hoping to find out."

"It's okay to be afraid. We all search for meaning at some point in our lives. Or at many points."

Chord knows she's right. He's scared to death.

She continues. "It all seems meaningless when we're young, because all that hard work eventually ends in death. Death is always following us."

Chord feels the hairs on the back of his neck tingle and a current run through his body, giving him a chill in the heat. "I just want to be happy."

"I have gas. There is enough to get you to the next station. But I ask a favor. Stay the night. I will make some soup, and then you boys sleep. Tomorrow you use the gas and continue on your discovery." She smiles. Her eyes hold a secret.

The old woman, the boy, and Manny peer in through the window of Chord's mind. His mind runs. *I don't know what I believe in. That is to say, I am uncertain of my faith. However, this place, this land, this woman's world, holds more than can be explained physically. As if she is a thousand years old and has seen the schematic for our world. I fear people who have such a sense of calm in such a harsh place. They make me feel weak and childlike. I wonder what Noah thinks. I wonder if his experience has numbed him to the glory of this woman. Or maybe he can see it with more clarity.*

"My husband and I moved to this land before we were married. His family and mine did not approve of our bond. Silly people. We grew the right plants to sustain us. We hunted snakes and lizards. I believe there are many gods. In a place like this, there have to be. My husband believed in only one. But I think he was just stubborn. I could not give him children. I'm sure that made him sad. But faith and love kept us strong. We never married the way he always said his family did. It didn't matter. We were united under the sun and moon. The spirits of my people and his. Sixty-one years we have lived here. Eight with just his spirit. I'm tired." Kachina motions to Noah. "You go now, Noah. The gas is under the trailer in canisters. I would like to speak with Chord alone."

"Yes, ma'am." Noah stands up and looks at Chord with a sense of pride.

Is he in on the secret? Chord thinks. Noah walks out.

"Your soul is twisted, Chord. Knotted up. You want to believe but can't. Your journey has meaning. But your happiness is like the snake in high grass. If I couldn't catch the snake, I would not survive here. I believe you are the one sent by the spirits to make right this final moon. Tomorrow you will bury me with my love. It is the last gift I can give to him. To follow his tradition." Kachina pauses and watches as Chord absorbs her words. "I see your thoughts and heart were not ready to hear these words. Please sit with me tonight. We will eat and trade stories. When the sun rises, you will find me and help me. This is my journey's end. I am happy."

Is knowingly letting someone take her life the same as killing her? I would've saved Manny if I could have. She has lived a full life. This is her choice. What's the other option? Guard her until we can get the car going and then let the authorities know? Put her away in some home? Isn't this her home? Chord just stares and doesn't speak aloud, and Kachina doesn't mind. She doesn't need him to speak, and Chord feels it.

Samantha sits in the café with her closed laptop on the table in front of her. She seems nervous. Her eyes scan the entrance. She undoes her ponytail and then affixes her hair into a messy top bun. She doesn't want to seem too put together, not that she feels at all together. With the nerves comes excitement as well.

After Samantha and Melissa initially spoke in the street, Samantha paid for a hotel room for Melissa to stay in. About four days passed, and Melissa reached out to set a date to sit down with Samantha to catch up.

You can share the same home, the same parents, and the same childhood, but sometimes that doesn't mean you know or understand any aspect of your sibling. How do people choose such different paths? Even with the knowledge that they will be hurting themselves or others.

Samantha waits. Melissa was supposed to meet her twenty minutes ago.

After waiting a full hour past the agreed meeting time, Samantha decides to go to the hotel where Melissa is staying. She walks up to the front desk and asks to dial the room number.

"Yes, ma'am. Who should I say is calling?"

"It's my sister. She might not be there, but we were supposed to meet. Samantha."

"Of course, ma'am." The employee dials, and someone answers. "Good morning, sir. I have a Samantha here to meet her sister."

Sir? A sinking feeling pulls the smile from Samantha's face.

"Yes, sir, I'll send her up." The employee looks to Samantha. "You can go right up. Suite sixty-four. It's on the sixth floor. Room four."

"Thank you." Samantha pushes the words out in an attempt to sound unaffected.

She enters the elevator as though walking into a cloud of sad energy. She presses the number six and wipes her eyes before the tears can reveal themselves. When the doors open, she turns down the hallway as if in a dream, as if she's walking down the hallway of their country home before her life was shattered by tragedy. The number four exposes itself; the door is slightly ajar. Samantha feels dread, but in that split second, she tries to imagine all the positive possibilities.

It is as though a tsunami of bleakness pours out from the door as it is opened by a shirtless man with an empty smile of three or four teeth; bloodshot, hollow eyes; and yellow-stained fingertips.

"Hey. You Samantha?" His breath smells.

"Where's Melissa?"

"Oh, she's just sleeping." He turns to look in the direction in which Melissa is sleeping, and Samantha pushes her way into the suite. She sees Melissa lying on the couch in front of a fireplace surrounded by white marble. On the table in front of her are hypodermic needles, torn baggies, blackened spoons, and spent tiny bottles of liquor. Samantha cries out Melissa's name.

Melissa wakes up as if in slow motion; a tourniquet is still loosely draped around her right arm. "Samantha?" Melissa looks at her with no emotion, barely even confusion. It's as if she isn't surprised, as if this were the only outcome she could imagine. "You want something to drink?"

"Melissa, what the fuck? We were supposed to meet! I thought you were done with this!"

Melissa comes into the reality of the moment but still emits no proper emotion for the present time. "What were you expecting?"

Samantha sinks even deeper than she already was. She can't form a sound. She slightly opens her mouth to respond, but nothing comes out. She looks at the ghastly, yellow-fingered, toothless creature who answered the door and then walks out.

The soup is made with snake and lizard meat and flavored with tules. It makes Chord feel as if he is part of the world, not just on it. Kachina seems pleased. There is quiet, calm joy.

Fear creeps into Chord's body as he watches her slip on her soup and smile. This woman has so much to offer this world. She is an example of wonder and glory, the last of her kind. Chord doesn't want to be responsible for the extinction of the humanity he sees in Kachina. *Decisions. The elusive snakes. Some moments just need to be enjoyed as they are, and then we move on.* Chord thinks of Samantha.

Some other moments should be developed and held on to. Put in an album to be relived.

"Do you boys like the soup?" Kachina looks at them and smiles. "It's an acquired taste, I suppose."

"It's great. Better than the slop in Afghanistan," Noah says.

Chord stares at Kachina. "How do you know about the woman and the boy? Do you see them?"

"I see what is in front of me. I know that my decision was made, and then you boys pulled up to my door, as if delivered to help me complete my journey."

"I was beat up by a couple of guys. I don't know why, but I was out, and they were protecting their neighborhood." Chord has never shared this information with anyone before. "They beat me good. I went back there. After I had healed and felt strong enough. I wanted to kill them. All I could do was hit the ground. They ran off screaming. I felt so free. My anger. Just free. Then I realized I wasn't. I had responsibilities. A job. Parents who loved me. A woman who, I think, felt something for me. With all that, I felt trapped. All that was good. But I felt free in rage."

Noah and Kachina listen to Chord with open minds and hearts.

"Then there was the truck driver. A monster within his desires. He was standing at the edge, begging for me to push him. I wanted to. I watched him plead for five minutes and then turn and sit in the sand, sobbing. I don't understand this place I'm in. Myself. My oldest friend took his life. There is so much death surrounding me. In such a short period of time." Chord focuses on Kachina. "What if I can't let this happen?"

Kachina smiles at Chord as if she knows the secret to life. "My heart beats, and my lungs welcome oxygen. Every sunrise is new. Every night sky holds wonder, and the wind chimes are always playing a different tune. I have loved. I have been loved. Every sound of wildlife or gentle breeze is a kiss from my husband. Children are born, and people die. That's where the glory hides."

Chord looks out the window, beyond the boy and the old woman, to the horizon. He looks at the red canyons, the orange sky, the white blotches artistically crafted and floating gently over the vastness, and the way their shadows dance on the warm sand.

"There it is."

Chord looks back to Kachina. Her face is orange, displaying wrinkled canyons of skin and bright eyes.

"We are all beset by fear and love and anger. By friends and enemies and family. By death. Be who you are. Let yourself go there. We all owe that to ourselves."

Ben and Samantha sit across from each other. A bottle of red wine is on the table.

"So what about your family?" Ben asks.

"What about them?"

"You never talk about your family. You live in the city alone. No pictures of your family. It's just interesting. Where did you get your loveliness from?"

"My parents died, and I inherited money." Samantha responds as if giving the sum of two plus two.

"I'm sorry. How old were you?"

"Seventeen." Samantha looks into her glass. A reflection

of herself looks back at her, red and dark. She sees that seventeen-year-old girl.

"I'm sorry."

"Don't be sorry. I have a sister, but she left when I was thirteen. She got into drugs, and you know how that goes. My parents basically disowned her. Then, when they died, she came around strung out, looking for money. Expecting it. But my parents didn't leave her anything. So naturally, she hated me. She tried to battle me for the money, but she would always show up in court high. The judge agreed to leave her the house. It only lasted two years, and then she lost that too. I went to NYU. Haven't seen her since." Samantha thinks of Melissa, her punching the glass, and the hotel room. She doesn't know why she lied to Ben. The relationship with her sister makes her feel flawed.

"I'm sorry. You're beautiful." Ben reaches across the table and grabs hold of Samantha's hand. "My brother and I were close. He left after high school. Not sure where he went. I just woke up, and he was gone. Every now and then, I would receive a letter from him, but they stopped too."

"Why did he leave?"

"He said the world was too big to stay in one place. I always wanted to travel. After he left, though, I felt like I had to be there for my parents. He was always the wild one. Instead of going away to school, I stayed." Ben drifts off with a longing in his eyes.

Samantha looks at Ben but thinks about Chord. *Why did he just leave? Some people need to keep moving to feel alive, while others just need some people.* She looks down at her reflection again and then back up at Ben, and for a moment, she sees Chord in his distant eyes.

Chord and Noah stand in front of the tombstone of Kachina's husband. Their hands and arms are spattered with dirt and sand. Their faces drip with sweat. Next to the tombstone is a hole large enough to fit Kachina. Next to the hole is the body.

"Let's get her in there. Gently." Noah climbs down into the hole and reaches up for the body.

Chord bends and slowly slides her into Noah's arms. They work together to make sure the blankets she is delicately wrapped in don't come loose. The last bit of the sun has risen over the horizon. It's an enormous, watchful eye glowing with power and beauty, a true creator of life.

Maybe that's what this is. Not death but birth. Reunited with love in an incandescent, more beautiful place.

With the body placed, Chord and Noah push the last few mounds of soil into position. "Should we say something?" Chords asks.

"Thanks for the gas. Hope you find your husband on your travels." Noah looks at Chord. "I'll get the car."

Chord stares down at Kachina's final resting place. "Thank you."

A snake slithers between Chord's legs, startling him, and moves off toward the rising sun. In the heat-hazy distance, Chord sees the silhouettes of Kachina, the gunshot boy, the old woman, and Manny. Kachina gathers them together. Her arms spread wide enough to embrace all of them. They look to Chord, smile, and turn into the light of the risen sun. A gentle breeze carries the quiet laughter of Samantha.

Chord smiles.

The car horn honks. "Let's roll!"

— 6 —

Chord pulls a piece of paper from his pants pocket. On it is Samantha's number. He's had it since he called home, but he hasn't had the courage to call her. He thinks of the cat and the morning he woke up next to her. It was peaceful, like the rising sun over the red canyons. He thinks of Manny. Manny knew what Chord was all about—phony, scared. That was the message he left. A cry for help—not for himself but for Chord. *Where are these fears born? Hatched from some subtle, subconscious egg.*

The headlights illuminate the first sign telling of New York. It glows like the eyes of a predator lurking in the shadow of night, surrounded by darkness. Chord isn't sure how to feel. They've been driving nonstop since Kachina. *Sometimes even vacations seem endless. Without a schedule and responsibility, we just don't feel whole. Without strings, a marionette is just a pile of wood.* Chord looks at Noah driving. He's focused, as if the delivery of Jose's ashes will be their deliverance. "What are your plans when you have no one else to deliver?"

Noah continues to look out into the darkness, the unforeseeable future. "I haven't delivered Jimmy."

"You did the best you could with Jimmy."

"That's what my lieutenant said." Noah's stare changes. He sees Jimmy drag himself from the burning wreck of their Humvee. His legs are mangled, with fire engulfing them. He's screaming for help. "I stopped to help some kids. One of their motorcycles broke down. They all told me not to stop. I knew I shouldn't have. Months of fighting. Killing. You can't see the good while you're there. It all seems senseless. I just wanted to help. Just a good deed that results in instant gratification. Bring some normalcy back to my unit. And they all died because of it. Then I killed those boys." Noah begins to sob. "I just want to go back and not stop. Just keep driving. I just want to keep driving."

Noah finally looks over to Chord. His face is wet with snot and tears. His eyes are wild with emotion. Chord grabs his head. The car stops on the interstate. Noah puts his head on Chord's shoulder and cries. The car rests, an insignificant vessel within a vast ocean of darkness on the road between salvation and regret.

The car is parked at a rest area. Chord stands next to a pay phone. With phone in hand, he begins dialing Samantha's number. He stops. He looks around the surrounding area, not sure what he is looking for. Part of him misses his ghoulish friends. It was as if they kept him on track. *You are who you surround yourself with.* He finishes dialing the number, and the phone rings. On the third ring, someone picks up.

"Hello?" Samantha's voice travels through Chord, electrifying his soul. "Hello?"

"Samantha."

"Chord? Is it you?"

"Samantha. I—" Chord can't seem to formulate words. At work, he can talk all night to complete strangers and help them come to a solution for their issues, but when he wants so deeply to express himself to a woman he cares for, he has no idea what to say.

"Chord, what happened to you? Why are you calling me now?"

"Samantha, I know that what I have to say—God, wait! I should've called you sooner. Always. I should've never stopped calling you. When we were apart, we should have just left the phones on so we could breathe together. I miss you. I've had this incredible—"

"Chord, stop." Samantha sits up on her couch, no longer frozen now that she's heard Chord's voice. Her eyes are sad. "What do you expect from me? This isn't some romance novel. I'm not the girl who waits and hopes for the good-guy-deep-down to find himself and then runs into his arms. I have a life. I deserve what you're spewing now. I deserved it before!" She sits back, as if she's been wanting to shout at the shadows of her life for a long time but never had the courage.

"You do. And I was crazy—am crazy. Just hear me. I should've called. Though I would've been no good for you a month ago. So I don't regret what has happened. Even if we never see each other again, I want you to know that you helped me understand I needed to make a change. You are the reason I need to be a better man."

Samantha sits up on the edge of the couch again.

"A couple of days ago, the sun was so profound. The world seemed to quiet down, and I heard your laughter. I'll be back in the city early tomorrow morning. I have to help a friend with something important, but tomorrow night, I'll be in our seat, guarding the back door. I hope to see you again in whatever capacity."

Samantha is once again frozen in place. The other end of the line cuts off. "Chord? Chord?" She pulls the phone away from her head and yells at it. "What the fuck?"

"Thanks for last night." Noah looks over to Chord. His bereaved eyes lack the hopefulness they had but seem a little more at peace.

"Oh, stop. You would've done the same for me. In fact, you saved my life in more ways than one. You're a good man."

"I never told anyone what happened that day. The guilt, man. The goddamned guilt. It's tearing me up. I see their faces every day." Noah looks out on the road. The traffic is getting heavier as they creep closer to the city. The sun has broken the horizon somewhere behind the trees and buildings. The world seems to have closed in on them. The horizon isn't far in the distance anymore but just ahead beyond the next structure.

"We had an interesting journey. One last delivery, and we're free. I called Samantha last night while you were sleeping."

"Good man. About time you grew a pair. What did she say?"

"Not much. She was pissed. I asked her to meet me tonight. I don't think I'll see her again."

"You never know."

"No, it's okay. I mean, I'm okay with it. Really, who do

I think I am? She's beautiful, smart, and funny. She doesn't have to sit around and wait on me."

"Yeah, she's probably better off. You're a moody bastard." Noah smiles at Chord.

Chord just smiles at the road.

The city is a hard place cut in concrete squares and littered with beauty—bold. The people are hardened but, like a calloused hand, still able to caress. There's diversity.

Chord picks the rearview mirror up off the floor and looks at himself. His eyes look tired. He has a scar on his upper lip. His skin is darkened from the sun. The city hasn't changed but feels different. There seems no quiet corner to rest.

"I don't know how anyone can live here." Noah looks over to Chord.

"I used to think I could. I wanted to." Chord remembers the quiet morning at Samantha's. *Sometimes we have to quiet our minds before we can find peace in our worlds.* "There are quiet places here. If you find them, you're lucky. Where are we heading?"

"It's about ten blocks up." Noah seems nervous for the first time since Chord met him.

"It's going to be okay, man. You've done something amazing with your life. You deserve to be proud."

It's too early to be awake, but Samantha can't sleep. Chord has invaded her life once again. She sits up in her bed and looks at the cat, who looks up at her, knowing it's too early to be awake. "What the hell was that? I mean, who does that?" Samantha looks at the cat as though it might answer. The cat purrs. "What am I gonna do?"

Noah and Chord stand on the sidewalk in front of their final destination, staring back at the car. It's as if they are both delaying the inevitable. "Okay, let's make this happen." Noah turns and walks into the building behind them.

"What about the urn?"

Noah smiles. "We don't need an urn this time."

Chord is perplexed.

Noah stares at him with a huge smile, as if he just asked the girl of his dreams for a date and she said yes. "Come. Trust me."

Chord looks back at the car one more time. "What about Jose?"

Noah just motions with his head for Chord to follow him. Chord does.

The door is freshly painted. The doorknobs and locks appear freshly polished. Noah stands in front of the door with his hand balled into a fist, held frozen at his shoulder, as if ready to knock. His other hand rises, and he drags his fingertips across the small name tag on the door: Salvino. He knocks.

Samantha sits at a café with her laptop open, staring at the screen.

> A phoenix rising from the flames,
> flames that now burn down the world that
> cradles me.
> You claim to be tamed,
> but these words and actions are the contrary.
> Such a brief jolt of time, a car crash,
> and you've made a wreck of me.

Samantha closes her laptop. She thinks of Chord. She thinks of Ben. *I have to tell him.* She packs away her laptop, leaps up, and races out the door.

Chord's parents sit at the table. There is no more nervous energy. They're calm. Their plates empty. Coffee steams in their mugs. The guitar stands in the corner of the room.

"Well, I have to read." Chord's mother stands up and begins clearing the table.

"Leave it. I'll clean it." Chord's father looks up at his wife with a joyful smile.

Chord's mother has recently joined a Realtor class. She smiles as she carries her book to the sofa. She hums the tune Chord's father always plays. *Sometimes starting over is a sign not of failure but of success. How much can we do with our lives? Who sets the limits other than ourselves?*

Noah knocks. The door opens.

"Banjoman!" Noah pushes inside and hugs the man who answers. "My brother, my man."

The man looks at Chord with shock and joy and closes his arms around Noah. "Noah?" The man holds Noah by the shoulders, steps back, and looks at his face. His eyes well up with shock and excitement. "Noah." He pulls Noah back in and squeezes him. He reaches out, grabs Chord with one arm, and pulls him in for a group hug. They all hug and smile and giggle like schoolboys. "What are you doing here, man? How'd you know where I was?"

"I wrote Aunt Mary after I was discharged. You seem to be doing well."

"Discharged?"

"Yeah." Noah turns his attention to Chord. "This is my hero, Chord." Tears of joy run down Noah's cheeks.

"So you're Jose?" Chord asks, looking at Noah with a smile of sincerity.

Noah smiles. "No, I'm Noah. The last to be delivered."

"Delivered?" the man asks.

Noah looks at Banjoman. "It's a long story."

"Well, come in! Close the door."

"So your brother's name is Banjoman?" Chord says.

Before they can move any farther into the apartment, there's a knock at the door, and Noah's brother goes to answer it.

Noah replies to Chord's question about his brother's name. "No, his name is Ben. But I always messed up saying the name Benjamin when I was younger. So it became Banjoman."

Ben stands at the open door, talking to whoever is in the hall. "You have to come in. My brother is here! I want you to meet him." Ben pulls the door open.

"Chord!"

"Samantha!"

"Ben?"

"Oh shit." Noah's eyes open wide. A smile slowly creeps onto his face.

Ben looks at Samantha with confusion. "You know him? What's going on here?"

"He's someone I ... Oh Jesus, Chord, what are you doing here? How? I mean, what?"

"I'm sorry. I just ... I mean, I don't ... I'm just going to go. It was nice to see you again. Noah, keep in touch; you have my info. Ben, it was a pleasure to meet you." Chord walks by Samantha. She smells good. Samantha stares at him, and he mouths, "Later." She smirks with her mouth still open from shock.

Chord walks down the hallway to the elevators. The apartment door shuts. While Chord waits for the elevator, the apartment door opens, and Noah runs out and down the hallway to Chord.

"Dude, that is pretty damn amazing! I'm certainly not going to be the third wheel on that conversation."

"I'm sorry I ruined your moment." Chord smiles.

Noah smiles back. "I feel really good, man. So that was Samantha? She's beautiful. Maybe if you or my brother can't hold on to her, I can take her out."

Chord looks at Noah. "You want to meet my parents?"

"Absolutely."

"Good, because I need a ride."

Samantha and Ben stand staring at each other. Samantha still hasn't moved from the spot where she first walked in.

"What just happened there?" he asks.

"Was that your brother?"

"Yes." Ben smiles. He hasn't stopped looking into Samantha's eyes. "But who was the other guy?"

Samantha gently smiles and looks down at her feet. *Love is like a really good movie that comes on late at night just before you go to sleep. You know you should just turn it off, but you stay up all night watching.* "That was Chord." *And it screws up your whole schedule.*

"You seem different. Happy. Like some weight has been lifted. I love to see you smile like that."

Samantha looks up at Ben, and he knows, and so does she now. She loves him. Ben smiles.

Noah's car pulls up in front of Chord's house. The lawn is freshly mowed. A wooden gate gently swings open and closed because Chord's father didn't close it all the way. Chord feels overwhelmed with emotion. There is such beauty in coming home to a place where you know you are loved unconditionally. It's as if everything Chord has taken for granted has flowed into his heart—memories of youth, love, his friendship with Manny, and his parents waiting to eat breakfast with him in the morning and dinner at night. The selfish behavior he's displayed over the past months makes him cringe.

"Nice house!"

"Yeah, it is. Surprised I wanted to leave it?"

"Hey, man, we all have our reasons."

Chord pushes open the passenger door, and it falls to the ground. They both laugh. Chord's smile becomes solemn. "It's kind of like you're delivering me too. Only I'm alive. Thanks to you."

Noah looks deep into Chord's eyes with his calming smile. "Thank you, Chord."

Chord's mother sits in the living room, studying. A gentle melody from an acoustic guitar is playing from Chord's parents' room. There is a knock on the door. Chord's mother folds the page of her book at the top corner to keep her place and walks to the door. She pulls open the door, and standing in front of her, as if a dream, is Chord.

"Chord!" She grabs hold of her son, and they embrace.

Chord's father stops strumming the guitar when he hears his wife scream and runs down the stairs to them.

"Chord! My boy." Chord's father opens his arms wide and hugs both of them, and Noah grabs hold of the Samson family and joins in on the hug. "Don't leave like that again. Please."

"I won't, Dad. I'm sorry for my behavior. I was ungrateful."

They all detach, and Chord's parents stand looking at Chord as if their view will keep him from ever leaving again.

"Well, let's go inside. Are you boys hungry?" Chord's mother looks at Noah and then back to Chord as if to remind Chord to introduce Noah.

"Oh yeah, this is Noah. He saved my life."

"We owe you then, Noah. Are you hungry?"

"I could eat."

Just like that, Chord and his parents are reunited. *This world could benefit from forgiveness. Maybe even a little humility. And love.*

The music is loud. The crowd is louder. *Sometimes it's easier to notice a change in yourself when you return to a place from your past that hasn't changed.* Chord thinks about the horizon and the red canyons. There at the end of the bar stands an old friend: a lonely chair waiting to be used, craving purpose. Chord walks over to his old companion and sits. He thinks, *How long do I wait? Will she show up? Ben seemed like a great guy.* He looks at the back door and smiles. He orders a beer.

Two empty glasses rest on the bar in front of Chord. He

has to use the bathroom but doesn't want to miss her if she walks in. The urge is great. The struggle is real.

Chord gets up fast and hurries to the bathroom. He stands at the urinal. The same battle of words and pictures on the wall greets him. He washes his hands. He notices they put a mirror in the bathroom. Chord looks at himself. He feels happiness—a little fear and maybe some doubt, but he's happy. Then, as he reaches for the door handle, he reads on the door, "Happiness is camouflage for despair."

If we trap our minds into believing we can't be happy, we never will. We have to surrender to the possibility of happiness, or we will forever trudge through despair. Chord is happy in this moment.

Chord exits the bathroom and sees, sitting in his chair, a warm smile and bright blue eyes. He smiles. "I didn't think you would come."

"I'm not sure what to think."

"There's always the back door."

Samantha smiles. "Why did you leave?"

"I'm not sure."

"Well, I know where I want to be. I know I'm scared. I know I'm not going to save you."

Chord looks at Samantha. Her face is austere and beautiful. "I was afraid I couldn't measure up to you. Afraid you deserved much more than I can give. I realize now that I was too self-involved and that you make me want to live happily ever after."

"Wow." Samantha looks down at her folded hands in her lap. She looks up at Chord. "That's the most amazing and the cheesiest thing I've ever heard!" She bursts into laughter. *How silly love is. How silly it makes us.*

They laugh, and the man sitting in the chair next to Samantha stands up and leaves. Chord sits down with Samantha. Their hands embrace. All the chairs are occupied.

Noah's car sits idling in front of Ben's apartment building. The car is clean. There's no more junk in the backseat. Sitting in the passenger seat is Jimmy's urn. Noah is behind the wheel. Ben comes out of his building with a suitcase. He looks down at his brother and the car waiting for him— adventure waiting for him. He thinks of Samantha. He might have lost her, but he has also gained. He is grateful.

"Just throw it in the trunk." Noah hits the trunk button and watches in the rearview mirror as his brother loads the suitcase. He smiles and looks over to the urn. "Where do you want to go, Jimmy? I'm thinking of a place where the horizon is vast and always in the distance and the wind carries magic." Noah moves the urn to the backseat, and Ben grabs the passenger door handle and pulls the door off the car. It falls to the ground.

"You've got to be kidding me."

"Just get in." Noah exits the vehicle and runs around to the passenger side to reattach the door. Then he runs back around and gets in.

"Okay, Noah, I'm ready for adventure. Where to?"

"If we knew that, it wouldn't be an adventure, big brother. The horizon holds the secret. You sure you're ready for this?"

"The world is too big to stay in one place."

They smile at each other, and the car putters off.

Chord's mother cooks for her family while reviewing a real estate study guide on the counter next to her. She's studying to earn her next certification. Chord's father strums his guitar and smiles at his wife, thinking about how lucky he is and watching her as she reads a bit of her study material and then moves back to the stove to move the food around the pan. His fingers stop strumming as he stares in awe of his amazing wife. *Such an amazing woman.*

She looks back at him. "What?"

"You're amazing."

She smiles. "Well, keep playing for me. I love your music."

Chord's father strums on.

Stolsky arrives home from work and sneaks in to put his bags down on the dining room table. He smells food and thinks it odd. He hears a giggle and then a "Sh!" from the kitchen. He smiles and sneaks over to the kitchen.

"Surprise!" his daughters shout out, and they laugh and run to him. "We made you French toast!"

Stolsky hugs them all and looks at his wife, who is standing by the table smiling, and he winks at her.

Becky Roberts watches her twins sleep, quietly sobbing, secretly looking at an old picture of Jimmy. She holds one of Jimmy's letters in her hand, and the rest are in a stack on the nightstand. Lying next to them is a Mass card with Jason's picture on it.

Samantha and Chord lay entwined together. The cat at the foot of the bed purrs. They kiss. Chord feels a sense of calm and wholeness.

—7—

Chord sits behind a small desk at the end of a long hallway in a dingy, lonely basement of the city court building. There are no windows, and there's a stale odor of human filth and garbage. Fluorescent lights flicker and hum over Chord. He watches a video on his phone.

Chord's father was able to save Chord's job by using some contacts he made when he was a police officer. Chord was suspended without pay for thirty days and had to agree to speak with the job psychologist for that time. When he returned to work, his weapon was taken for safekeeping, and he was placed on modified duty in central booking, where people who are arrested come to be turned over to the Department of Corrections and wait to see a judge.

Chord thinks about Noah and Ben, the road, and the world. The contrast between the freedoms he felt then and the confinement he feels now is enough to drive anyone mad. He thinks of Kachina and of Samantha. Chord's phone vibrates, and the video pauses itself. It's a message from Samantha: "Hang in there, baby! I know it's hard, but I love you." Chord smiles. It's as if she can read his mind.

Just then, a police officer walks up to Chord's desk. He

hands Chord some paperwork. Chord reads the name of the prisoner: Melissa Allman. He looks at the officer and then over to the newly arrested woman. "Do you have a sister?"

Melissa doesn't respond. She stares at the floor as if she is balancing on a rock floating in lava.

"Miss?"

The officer guarding Melissa gently shakes her shoulder, and she looks up at Chord and says, "What?"

"Do you have a sister?"

Melissa looks at Chord. She looks through him, as if the answer is behind him. "We're all alone in this world."

Chord directs his attention to the officer. "What did you pick her up on?"

"She's a crackhead. She assaulted her dealer with a brick. Fucked him up pretty bad."

Chord looks back to Melissa with a helpless look in his eyes.

Chord exits the building and squints in the light of the day. Sometimes he forgets the sun is still out. He no longer works the midnight shift, so he has the rest of the day to himself. He walks in the light of the sun, in the city that holds so much turmoil and glory, hope and fear, anguish and joy. He walks. His life is like this city, dark and light, cold and hot, hard and unforgiving yet full of possibility. He walks home—to Samantha.

Noah and Ben speed toward the bright orange sun resting on the horizon. The vastness surrounds them and cradles them. Ben looks out at the world like a mother looking at her child for the first time. He feels freedom, fear, and happiness.

Noah pulls over and stops at the side of the road.

Ben curiously looks at him.

"This is the spot. It's time." Noah reaches back and grabs the urn holding Jimmy's remains. "Come on."

Ben follows Noah out to the edge of the red canyon overlooking the fiery orange ball floating just above the earth. Noah pours Jimmy out into the breeze. It's as if the ash takes on the color of the sun, and Jimmy's soul is revealed on its final journey home.

EPILOGUE

A hundred-watt bulb fires on, illuminating a modern-styled bathroom. A man in his late forties enters and urinates in the stainless-steel bowl. When he finishes, he stands over the sink and runs hot water over his hands. His hair is thick and black, with chunks of gray scattered about. He cups his hands to collect a small pool of water, which he then puts his face into. He's a slender man in fine physical condition. He reaches for the towel beside the vanity and dabs his face dry. He looks at himself in the mirror, staring deep within himself.

Who is he? Chord Samson. His face is still chiseled yet aged. He hears a knock at the door, followed by a little girl's voice.

"Daddy, dinner's ready! Mom says it's getting cold!"

Chord pulls the door open quickly, startling his beautiful daughter. He grabs her and swings her up over his head, draping her small body over his shoulder. "Well, let's get downstairs before Mom yells at me!"

His daughter laughs, and they run down the stairs to the dining room.

Samantha smiles, and her bright blue eyes light up as Chord enters the room with their daughter. Chord's parents, now an elderly couple, smile as well. They sit at the table, waiting to start dinner.

Chord retired a few years early from the police force after he and Samantha married. His novel, or secret autobiography, reached the best-seller list, and there has been talk of it being adapted into a film. *Just like any war, the small battles of life chisel and mold people into adulthood.*

Chord walks over to the dining room window. As he reaches for the curtain, he looks out into the night. Standing on the lawn is an old man with a peaceful, calm smile. Chord thinks of the old woman and the boy. He thinks of Manny and the road. It seems so long ago now.

Behind him, he hears his family settling in around the dinner table, serving each other food, and the clang of metal utensils on glassware. He smells the aroma of a scented candle mixed with food. He sees the white picket fence bordering their front lawn. He puts his hand to the glass window pane. It's cold, as if an invisible barrier from some outside world.

Chord turns and sits at the head of the table with his back toward the window. He looks at each member of his family and smiles. In the corner of the room rests an acoustic guitar. Hanging on the wall, alongside pictures of Chord, Samantha, and their family, is the musical-note frame displaying photos of Chord and his young father side by side in uniform. *Harmony.*

Chord smiles on. His mind is full of thoughts. *We are all beset by life's inscrutable nature.*